Mr Robbins

Mr Robbins

Neil Jeffery

2014

First Printing: 2014

This book was first published in 2012 by Neil Jeffery as "The Curtain" by Fiona Robbins in a slightly different form.

ISBN 978-1-291-86348-2

This edition first published in 2014 by Neil Jeffery

Cover design Copyright 2014 Martyn Jeffery

Cover image "Beachy Head 2" is used with permission. Copyright Daniel Nork

"Glue" is used with permission. Copyright 2012 Lisa von Hasenberg

£1 from the sale of each copy of this novel will be donated directly to Pancreatic Cancer Action (UK Registered Charity No. 1137689)

Dedication

In memory of Mo

Contents

Acknowledgements

I would like to thank many people for their help and support in the publishing of this novel.

The staff and supporters of Pancreatic Cancer Action, a UK charity that is seeking more research on early diagnosis of such a pernicious illness – you guys are amazingly indefatigable – the purple army will win in the end!

To my daughters and the rest of my family – thank you as ever. I don't think that I thank you enough for all your love and support.

Many thanks to my cousin Martyn Jeffery for creating the cover to this novel, and to Daniel Nork for kindly allowing us to use his stunning photograph.

Many thanks to LisavonH for allowing me to use the words to such a beautiful and appropriate song.

Part One - Beginnings

Up At The Head

I don't really care for one moment how many people disagree with me, but I think there is nowhere better to go and be alone with your thoughts than the English countryside. Sure, I have visited some beautiful places in the world – Barcelona, the Grand Canyon, Venice, Berlin, even, but they are all so very *busy*. What I crave in this life, and what I will crave until my dying day, is the ability to actually sit and be alone with my thoughts, my mind, myself, and especially at those times when I feel I physically need to do so, and let me tell you, on that cold, blustery day in March, I really needed to do so. I should really introduce myself at this stage but, quite frankly, at the moment I can't actually be arsed to do so. I crave your indulgence, but I hope you'll understand my reasons in time, particularly as I think back to that time of my life.

I am a son of the South, and will always be so. I spent my formative years in the idyllic small-town atmosphere of the town of Cranbrook in the Kentish Weald, a lovely small market town overlooked by a large windmill, and over the years I moved around as I reached adulthood – university in the badlands of Surrey where I learned the dark arts of accountancy (fret not, this isn't a story about my misadventures in the accounts department of a multinational company, even if it might give a new slant to the phrase 'double entry'), and then moving to the Sussex countryside – to the outskirts of a pleasant, if slightly, run-down, seaside town, from where I indulged my principal passions – cricket, real ale (the local best bitter in East Sussex is the best I have ever tasted), family, friends and generally enjoying a restful existence.

Oh sod it, I'd best tell you my name, I suppose, even if we are not all that well acquainted yet. My name is Peter Robbins, and I am a 44 year-old divorced father of three children, who are fifteen, thirteen and nine. You'll meet them a bit later, I hope, so please stick with me. You may have already noticed, by the way, that I have a slightly subversive tone – fact is that I have found the one sure fire remedy for a stressful existence is to stick up a single digit to life and say 'bugger it!', but not when my kids are around, though, as I never bloody well swear when they are around me, and it's to my constant regret that I don't see them as often as I should. You see, real life sometimes gets in the way, doesn't it?

Anyway, where was I? If you drive along the coast road in East Sussex – the nice parts, I mean, not bloody Brighton – in a westerly direction, you go through some very pleasant and not so pleasant places. Hastings, I mean, has seen better days, but if you carry on you get to the genteel calmness of Bexhill-on-Sea with its lovely art-deco arts centre, the De La Warr Pavilion, thence on to Little Common, Pevensey and the old-aged, Werthers Originals-soaked charm of Eastbourne, a town I loved to visit with my family when I was a nipper. Eastbourne was always a bit strange for a young child, as it always seemed so full of old people. I used to joke to my family that people lived in Eastbourne until they died, and then they were allowed to move to Bexhill. Anyway, I digress. Driving along Eastbourne seafront you pass the pier and the Wish tower (what you wish for I have no idea – maybe for warmer temperatures, I guess), and from there the road heads up a hill slightly and then, after a while it meanders up the hill and onto the verdant majesty of the South Downs.

Yes, I admit it, I am in love with the Downs, because there are few places down that way that you can actually get away from civilisation, which is exactly what I wanted to do that morning, I drove along the seafront and turned left and headed towards Beachy Head. Once I got there I parked my car (in case it's blocking your vehicle in the car park it's the blue Volvo S80). I walked out onto the open green expanse, past the telephone call box with the prominent advertisement for The Samaritans, and plonked myself down about ten feet from the cliff edge, unzipped my bag and took out a bottle of Blue Label ale. I fished around for an inordinate amount of time for a bottle opener because, let's face it, you can never find these bloody things when you really need them, can you? However, when I found it I opened the bottle and took a long sip of the nectar inside, and closed my eyes, and lay back on the grass to rest and take in the wondrous silence.

Don't bloody well ask me how long I slept for, because I haven't got the foggiest idea. I dreamt of nothing in particular, but when I awoke, when my eyes opened and I got accustomed to the faint sunlight that was twinkling through what had earlier been a slate-grey sky, I was totally taken aback to see a face peering over me. It had clear, sparkly eyes, and it made me jump, particularly when its whiskers tickled my stubbly face and it gave my nose a good lick! No, my luck wasn't suddenly in – the face belonged to what appeared to be a very boisterous and extremely friendly yellow Labrador that appeared to be about 4 years old. I smiled as my mind was cast back to the family mutt we had had when I was a little boy, but my restful contentment was broken by a shrill female voice with a very distinctive Irish accent.

"Seamus, where *are* you? Bugger me, Seamus, that's not your average suicide jockey now, is it, boy?!"

Moments when life turns on its head

Before you ask me, I haven't got a bloody clue when all this madness started. Well, actually, that'd be a lie, but I want to explain it properly and clearly, and I never ever use ten words when one hundred of the little blighters will suffice. I'd been taking my annual leave, resting and catching up with my ever-growing pile of unread emails. One Sunday morning, a few weeks beforehand, I suddenly had cause to sit back in my office chair, take off my reading glasses and wince. I suddenly had what felt like some bastard sticking a knife into my midriff. That sodding knife went straight through my abdomen to right between my shoulder blades. Now I will say right now that I am by no means what you could call a wimp – I am six foot four and built like a brick shithouse – but it was all I could do to simply sit there, passively, while the pain shot right through me for what seemed like an eternity, and all I could do was sit there, sit and wait for it to subside, sit there and take simple deep breaths.

As soon as it came, the pain subsided. If I were to be honest I'd say it lasted ten to fifteen minutes, and as soon as it came it went. I sat up, shook my head, wiped the tears from my eyes and walked into the kitchen to make a cup of coffee. In many ways that period of excruciating pain served as an effective alarm clock, as I suddenly remembered that the kids, Ellen, Lizzy and Peter, were being brought over by my ex so I could have Sunday lunch with them. All I can say is thank Christ for supermarkets and Sunday opening!

Three days later I found myself sat in the waiting room at the Doctor's surgery. Bugger me, but they are depressing places, aren't they? All you can sense there is the stench of sick people, and I bet you can catch loads of things there. Bubonic plague, amoebic dysentery and chicken pox are sure fire probables – I dare say the only things you cannot normally catch are syphilis and galloping knob-rot, well if you don't do anything you shouldn't! Anyway, after sitting around for what seemed like an eternity, I found myself in the consulting room of Dr Matthews, my favourite GP. He's a robust, no-nonsense old-fashioned doctor. None of this farting around and beating around the bush for Dr Matthews, no sir!

"So, Peter, to what do I owe this pleasure? I must say, I don't see you all that often,"

"Hello, Doc, I'm sorry to bugger up your schedules by turning up. It's probably nothing, but…"

"Oh shit, I hate those words! Right, what's up, mush?"

And so I spent a little bit of time telling the plain-speaking doctor about my assignation with the 'phantom impaler' on Sunday morning. This was accompanied by sundry 'oohs' and 'aahs' from my partner in this conversation. He enquired about my general lifestyle, asking if I was still an inveterate smoker.

"So, how many coffin nails per day?"

"Oh, about twenty, I guess"

"Right, let's put that down as thirty then, eh?" he said, giving me a sly wink that made me realise that he knew me all too well. He then checked my chest with what seemed to be the world's coldest stethoscope, made a few notes and told me that he wanted me to get checked out at the local slaughterhouse, I mean, hospital. So the next stage was then a trip to the hospital. Not in a few weeks, but in a couple of days. Still, nothing to worry about, eh?

The medics at the hospital haven't got much of a sense of humour, have they? They are chatty, don't get me wrong, but maybe they didn't appreciate my sense of humour. When I was asked if I was allergic to anything, my reply of "well, I am sensitive to criticism" was met with a friendly smile rather than a genuine laugh. I can never tell if it's my crap jokes or they are just miserable bastards. Anyway, after the most boring white-knuckle ride of all time, in a CT scanner, I found myself sat in a gown watching as the whole of the medical profession sped past me, seemingly ignoring me. It's probably the shit humour that does it. Eventually a registrar came up to me and pulled the curtains around my cubicle. I hopped up on to the bed and had my abdomen prodded a little more. Maybe it's the fact that it has a malleable quality akin to plasticine that it seemed to have such an appeal. I was about to offer the doctor a prize if he could fashion my stomach into a likeness of Homer Simpson when he stopped what he was doing, picked up my notes, and spoke to me in a strangely hushed tone.

When I finally got the chance to put my trousers back on and step out into the open-air I suddenly noticed the sound of the birds up in the oak tree in the hospital grounds. If it wasn't for the fact that it was a bunch of bloody crows I might have deemed it as strangely mystical. I walked over to my car, my trusty Volvo, got in and sat down in the comfy leather seat that had become gloriously moulded to the shape of my arse over the years, put my head back on the headrest, and I wept. I wept like there was no tomorrow. Torrents of tears streamed down my face and I suddenly looked like I was suffering from the world's worst head cold – a bright red streaming nose and eyes that looked like Christopher Lee in one of my favourite old Hammer horror movies. My mind was spinning – I wasn't sure what I should do next. Should I go and see the kids? I desperately wanted to see them, but I didn't want them to see their old dad looking like he had been smacked in the knackers with a sledgehammer.

I suddenly felt my phone vibrating in my breast pocket. My first thought was to ignore it, but then I made the mistake of checking to see who it was. It was my mother – who had always had a happy knack of ringing me at completely the wrong time. I answered and tried my utmost to make out I was ok. My snivelly tone was put down to suffering from a particularly deadly bout of manflu – so bad that I had imposed a 30 mile exclusion zone around my house to make sure I didn't infect the rest of mankind and cause the demise of modern society as we know it. You know that kind of thing. I promised I would go and visit her in her little flat in Tunbridge Wells when I was feeling better and managed to end the conversation in what was a personal best of four minutes and forty-seven seconds.

My family has a trait of indulging in some of the most plain-speaking streams of consciousness in existence. Indeed you might have noticed that I am somewhat forthright in my language. Anyway, after a couple more minutes of sober introspection, and I didn't plan on remaining sober for long once I had got home, I simply said to myself, "right, you daft bastard, get it sorted and get yourself home", turned the key in the ignition, slipped the gearstick into Drive and drove home. There, I felt certain, I would be able to draw up a plan of attack!

Who needs antimacassars in the 21st Century?

It's strange, but I lay there up by the cliff's edge for a little while longer, even if that ever so friendly dog was beginning to drool over me, but at least it was friendly contact.

"So, are you going to jump, or are you going to let my dog lick you to death?"

"Sorry, I got carried away and transported to a bygone age," I said, wiping canine saliva off my face, with a smile.

"Well, I hope that doesn't mean you spent your past having unnatural relationships with dogs!" said this straight-talking dog owner.

"No, not at all."

"Good, 'cos that would be pretty low."

"No, low would be a chihuahua."

I looked up, and took a good look at the woman whose pet had interrupted my sleep. She wasn't what you would call a classical beauty by any stretch of the imagination. She was quite tall – well from what I could judge lying back on the grass – and she was wearing a pair of purple Doc Martens with a flowery, floaty-style skirt. Over her top was a green waxed jacket. She had a thin face with quietly-defined, chiselled features. A pair of pink spectacles was perched on her nose, although she seemed to be looking over them as she gazed down at this nutter that Seamus was getting to know very well. Atop her head was an unruly mass of curly red hair.

"My name's Fiona, Fiona Mulgrew. So, tell me, young man, do you come here often? If so, why haven't you jumped yet?"

I wasn't exactly sure how to answer. I gave a couple of non-committal grunts, which hopefully gave the impression that the one thing I most dearly wanted in all the world was to be left alone, but I failed. The next thing I knew was that those bloody Doc Martens were sitting beside me on the grass, and that as Fiona sat I spied that she was wearing a pair of scarlet woollen socks that rippled over the top of her boots. She certainly didn't dress to impress!

"Sure, don't talk to me if you don't want to, but I am sure that you don't want to be drinking that beer on your own, do you now?" Fiona pointed towards the empty bottle of Blue Label at my feet. "You don't by any chance have a spare bottle you're willing to share, do you?" I fumbled inside my bag and pulled out a second bottle, removed the lid, took a swig and offered her the bottle. "Sure, I just knew you'd never be settled with just the one, would you?" Fiona smiled, and I couldn't help but notice the fact that she had a smile that seemed to brighten that gloomy day, with gleaming brilliantly white teeth.

Time certainly flies when you are having fun, doesn't it? In no more than what felt like half an hour, the sky was filled with a milky twilight. I glanced at my watch and saw that it was past five o'clock. Sheesh! In the past few hours I had done nothing more than indulge in very light-hearted, very silly conversation with Fiona. Conversation topics included dogs, which seemed entirely appropriate as Seamus was lying obediently at Fiona's side, apparently sleeping off the morning's exertions, the best place to get a curry in Croydon and, believe it or not, my sainted Aunt Maud, whom I hadn't seen in absolute yonks and who lived in a warden-assisted flat in Burgess Hill. I am not entirely sure that I wanted the conversation to end.

"I don't know about you, but my arse has gone to sleep," Fiona mentioned as a chilly breeze cut across us, "d'you fancy a cuppa back at mine?" She was gingerly lifting herself off of the grass, and gave Seamus a little nudge to wake him up. "Daft fecking dog, aren't you? Come on, time to go home, boy!"

"But you have only just met me."

"Sure, but you don't look like an axe murderer."

"Do you know what psychopathic axe murderers look like?"

"Well no, but you look honest."

It transpired that they lived in a little flat in the Meads area of Eastbourne, a pleasant suburb full of Victorian houses with high ceilings and enormous rooms. Instead of relying on Fiona to walk down the hill, I offered her and the dog a lift in my car. This was a fatal error as, as soon as he leapt on to the back seat of the Volvo, Seamus had upended a buff-coloured file that had contained my credit card and bank statements and had started chewing a reminder letter to me from those nice people at Barclaycard. This dog had taste! The drive took about ten minutes until we arrived outside Fiona's first floor flat. She took out her key and turned to me.

"I must say that this *is* strictly a cuppa, I certainly don't do euphemisms, and secondly I am not going to apologise for the state of the flat. You take me as you find me, okay?" I nodded silently.

She certainly wasn't wrong! Inside the flat looked as if it had been hit by a particularly effective nuclear device. There were bookcases groaning under the weight of hundreds of books, a floor littered with sundry pieces of paper, an artist's easel by the window, a small desk that was home to what appeared to be an antique laptop computer, and most strikingly the radiators had been decorated by a festival of laundry – t-shirts, skirts, jumpers, knickers of all styles and bras. Anything that might have originally been the purest white was now tinged with a used, grey hue. I wasn't complaining, having never been the tidiest of souls myself. This flat looked lived in, adored, and loved in, and it warmed my heart and brought a smile to my often all too serious face.

All of a sudden the sound of crashing crockery was followed by a cry of "Jesus Mary and fecking Joseph!". I dashed into the kitchen and could see that a pile of washing up on the drainer had slipped and two coffee mugs had been knocked onto the tiled floor, where they had smashed. Fiona was clutching onto an assorted collection of plates of all sizes, desperately trying to stop them falling and meeting a similar fate to the mugs. Now I know that dogs cannot speak, but Seamus was sitting there in his basket with what appeared to be an expression that said something along the lines of 'business as usual, then'. I helped Fiona salvage the teetering stockpile.

"Now, you see, I only have two coffee cups and they're both smashed to smithereens, so they are. Do you want a beer instead?"

"Depends on the beer, I suppose. I am a fussy sod."

"I bet you are. Let's have a look, then, shall we?" Fiona stepped through a pile of washing that had not yet made its way into the washing machine that stood not two feet from it. She opened a cupboard, and deftly caught a packet of microwave rice that immediately fell out, and then picked out a couple of brown, glass bottles. At least she didn't refrigerate bitter. I hate that.

"How does Old Speckled Hen sound?" This was not a bad option, not by a long chalk.

Once I had been handed a glass of bitter, I walked back into the lounge and sat down on the large, well-used brown leather sofa. It was so well used that my knees were immediately on a similar level to my head. I was, though, sitting, which was good. I sipped my beer, and gave a huge sigh of contentment. My hostess came into the room and walked over to the office chair that stood beside the desk. She lifted up a pile of papers from the seat and unceremoniously dropped them on the floor. She sat down, swung round in the chair, taking a sip from her glass, and made her opening gambit.

"Now then, Eeyore, you don't say much about yourself do you?"

"Why call me Eeyore?"

"'Cause you always look so fecking serious and miserable. Sure now, life is to be lived, not endured. What's so shitty about your life that you can't smile about it? I've got supplies. Tell me about yourself. Sure, if you take more than a week I'll have to ring the Red Cross for food parcels, but don't worry, I have my own personal hotline!"

I gave a weak smile, and started to tell her all about myself, and my life. But where to start? I insisted to Fiona that, the moment she became bored, she should indicate as such. She assured me she would, and said a probable signal would be her snoring in her chair. I took a deep breath, and began.

I tried to be positive about everything. I spoke of an idyllic childhood in the High Weald, growing up as the second of three children. I tried to speak warmly of my elder sister and younger brother even if, over the years, relations between us had been somewhat strained from time to time. I talked about my parents.

Sheila, my mum, had been a school cook and my dad, Eric, the man from whom I had inherited my tendency to be plain-speaking, had died fifteen years ago at the age of sixty-eight. He'd been a bricklayer and had a very dry sense of humour. He wasn't averse to colourful language, and it had been from him that I had broadened my vocabulary of obscene and scatological terms. They say imitation is the sincerest form of flattery but, as a youngster repeating those words, he had often given me a clip round the ear. Fiona chuckled and asked me to offer some examples of what I actually classed as 'choice' vocabulary, but, suddenly embarrassed, I declined politely.

I glossed over my marriage, which had ended seven years earlier, but I did warmly harken back to the day that Ellen, my eldest child, had been born after a difficult labour, how I had been such a gibbering wreck that the nurses had banned me from the delivery room, fearing that I might accidentally pull the pipe that carried the entonox away from the wall. As I wanted to create a good impression to Fiona, I explained that I had smartened up my act with Lizzy and Peter's births, and had merely accidentally tipped a glass of water over my ex-wife's head when I mistimed offering her refreshment during a particularly long contraction way back in 1999. At this admission Fiona howled with laughter and nearly dropped her glass, something that made her laugh even more.

Fiona looked down at the ale in her glass, paused for a second, and then looked up at me, this time with quite a serious look on her face.

"So why were you up at Beachy Head getting pissed? What's wrong? I mean, you seem like a level-headed kind of guy. Were you going to jump?"

"Oh, shit no," I said in a dismissive manner, failing to meet Fiona's gaze, "I was just taking the day off from work because I..."

"Bullshit! I can sense trouble a mile off, and besides I saw an NHS letterhead in the back of your car. Call me psychic. Well, that and the packet of industrial-strength painkillers in your jacket pocket. Either you aren't feeling well or you were planning on knocking out a pair of baby elephants on your way home."

"You don't miss a trick, do you?" I said, smiling across the room at my new-found friend, who clearly had the measure of me. I could see that I had best spill the beans, as it were. The very nice registrar at the hospital had told me that the CT scanner had located something in my abdomen that shouldn't be there. To be precise there appeared to be a mass in the region of my pancreas. I hate it when they use words like 'mass'. Why don't they use words like 'lump' or 'tumour'? They are far more emphatic, far more definitive, far more, and even though I hated this word at that moment, far more final.

The doctor hadn't stopped at that point, though. It was a given that the hospital wanted to remove a section for biopsy. Apparently this procedure could be done via a laparoscopy, and the results would be available within a week. There was an additional snag, though. As if a tumour attached to my pancreas wasn't enough, there appeared also to be small, additional tumours on my liver. This meant that, in all probability, if it was what they were suspecting, it had not been caught at an early stage.

"So tell me, do you have cancer, then?" Fiona didn't seem to waffle about, which was a good thing, as it focused my mind.

"Well, to tell the truth, I don't know yet."

"Why the hell not?"

"Well the sample was taken for biopsy last week. I had the procedure done last week. I could show you my scar, but I'd have to marry you afterwards," I smiled, weakly, in an attempt to put Fiona at her ease. I needn't have worried.

"No, you're okay there, you silly fecker! So when do you find out?"

"I should have gone in today, but I couldn't face the knowing"

"The knowing?"

"Yes, you know, the knowing. Whether I have, you know, *it*"

"*It*?"

"You know!"

"Maybe I do, maybe I don't, but I want to hear *you* say it. What's *it*?"

"Oh you do, do you?" I was more than a little annoyed at this stage, "whether I have the big C... you know, cancer". I sat back on the sofa, relieved at having said the word that had been taboo for me for such a long time, and immediately my arse dropped a little further in the ever so soft upholstery. I rested my head back, then I put my hand behind my head and touched something odd – from behind my head I pulled out something I hadn't seen since the days when I visited my gran in Uckfield when I was a child.

"Who the hell uses antimacassars in the twenty-first century?"

"I do. I'd tell you why, but I'd have to marry you afterwards."
Fiona smiled and poured me another beer.

Crazy Diamonds

As the evening went on, Fiona refused to allow me to wallow in a sea of my own misery. As a hostess, she was kind, generous and unstinting in her hospitality. Sadly, our supplies of beer ran out in a couple of hours, so we had to adjourn to the off-licence at the supermarket to pick up fresh supplies. Now, I am not often given to taking pride in my so-called 'masculinity', but as a man in his forties who is waiting on a potential death sentence from a pernicious and extremely painful disease, I felt proud to have a younger woman like Fiona walking alongside me to the shop and back.

Once we got back it was Fiona's turn to tell me a bit of her life story. Originally from County Wicklow, she'd come over to the England at nineteen when her parents, as she put it, 'asked her to leave home' to study at Winchester College of Art, hence the easel. I asked her with, I admit, a wink of my eye, to show me her portfolio, but all that elicited was a slap on the wrist. Eastbourne had become Fiona's hometown after she had married an itinerant session musician from Ringmer at the age of twenty-three. The marriage had not provided any issue, apart from Seamus, and she and her husband had separated, and subsequently divorced three years previously, when it transpired that her husband's regular gigs in London had also included the unforeseen benefit for him of him servicing a trombonist from Notting Hill. I suddenly felt a little odd being in the company of a woman fifteen years my junior, as if there was something morally wrong with talking to a much younger woman. I instinctively looked at my watch.

"Oh you're fine there, Eeyore. You don't have to go anywhere, do you? I can make a bed up for you on the sofa."

"Well, that's very kind of you. Only if it's not too much trouble."

"Well, you can see how much trouble I usually go to. When I said make a bed up, I meant throw a duvet and pillow at your head."

"Oh, that's alright then." I smiled, and Fiona smiled back. We carried on chatting. We rang up for a pizza delivery, which was uneventful but for the fact that Seamus appeared to love pepperoni, and olives, and tomatoes, and cheese, and pretty much anything else he could lay his paws on. After his supper, Seamus jumped up on to the sofa next to me, gave me the filthiest of looks, which inferred to me that I was, in fact, sitting in his space, and sat down, his head resting upon my thigh, eyes looking up at me, saying 'you bastard!' At this point Fiona fired up her laptop and asked me what kind of music I liked. I think that this must have been a rhetorical question, as she had obviously chosen what she wanted to listen to. Fortunately for me I was extremely pleased to hear the strains of Pink Floyd playing 'Shine on you Crazy Diamond'.

Well, that was it. No sooner did I hear those words than something was triggered in my subconscious that led to a single solitary tear running down my face. It's something that happens with me. I try to be assured, calm and collected in public, but if there is a song, a television programme or even a film that evokes a certain memory or emotion at any time of day, I cry. It's what I would deem to be the weakest aspect of my character. It can be embarrassing, because my subconscious hasn't learned to be all too discerning when it comes to the company I am keeping when this happens. On one particularly shaming occasion I was sat in the TV room in halls at university watching 'Neighbours' (please don't condemn me for this), when Bouncer, the Ramsey Street dog was hit by a car and was lying helpless in the street. The next thing I knew was that my most hard-drinking friends from the university rugby club had chosen that exact moment to step into the room for the first time in their university careers. Well, let me tell you, that was a hard one to live down, especially when our opponents in the very next game wore cut-outs of the Andrex puppy on their shirts, solely to take the piss out of me.

Anyway, back to the present, and Fiona gave a sigh of what I can only call faux-exasperation, got up and walked over to the sofa and sat down beside me. She put an arm round me and just sat there, holding me, until I could regain my composure. This was a very intimate, yet totally asexual moment. What I mean by this was that, even though I was being cuddled by a fairly attractive younger woman, whose contours I could feel shaping themselves around mine, it had been such a long, long time since anything like this had happened to me that I could not, and did not want to respond in any way. This wasn't the time, or the place, and besides Seamus had decided to advance along the sofa so he was trying to lie down on the sofa in that infinitesimally small gap behind Fiona and myself.

As the final strains of the guitar solo on the song started to fade into the distance, Fiona chose to break the silence gently, whilst still holding me.

"So, Eeyore, I tell you what you are going to do. Tomorrow you are going to ring the hospital to find out what the news is. Then you are going to take the news in, remain as calm as possible, and then go and see your kids. Sure I'll come with you, but mainly as travelling company. I can take Seamus for a walk or something while you are seeing them. You can choose how much, or how little, you tell the kids, but you owe it to them, and yourself, to see them. I could see how much they gladden your heart when you spoke about them earlier. From there, we can work out what to do next."

"You'd do that for me? You hardly know me!"

"I think I know you better now than most people, don't you think?"

I admitted that, once again, Fiona was correct. I smiled weakly, and had even become used to the stupid nickname she had given me.

"So if, and it's a possible, not a probable if, I go along with your suggestion, what do you get out of it all. Where's the quid pro quo here?"

"Ah, well you see young man, I love to do portraits. For a while now I haven't had any willing subjects to sit for me. Poor old Seamus has been a substitute, but I can now do dog portraits with my eyes closed. I want a new, interesting, and human subject to study. I'd like, if possible, to do a series of pencil sketches of you. Yeah, I want you to be my muse…"

Unaccustomed as I was to being anyone's muse, I had a think for a moment or two. I asked whether Fiona would want me to pose doing anything in particular, to which the answer was a resounding no. All she wanted was to be able to sketch me as I went about my daily life. I would be able to check, vet, and even veto sketches at the end, but she did want to, maybe, eventually display them in an exhibition. 'Life' would be the overarching title, apparently. This proved to be scarily ironic, as there was the distinct possibility that mine might come to a premature end a little earlier than I had planned.

"It's getting late now, Eeyore," said Fiona. She found me some bedding which, as promised, she threw at me, accompanied with a girlish giggle. She then bent over me, kissed me on the forehead, and left the room, "sweet dreams!"

Mr Silly's guide to life

Early the next morning I woke to the sound of shuffling footsteps. It was barely light in the lounge, and I heard Fiona walking towards the room. The first thing I saw when I opened my eyes was a pair of very pale, very slender, but also very long legs, that stretched up inside a greying white jersey nightie. For decency's sake I didn't dare look up any further, so I looked down and saw a pair of dark grey woollen bed-socks and a pair of pink fluffy slippers.

"Morning, sleepyhead! How you doing today? I'm afraid coffee and tea are still off the menu, but I can do you toast and orange juice. That is, if it hasn't gone off!" Fiona smiled at me and turned round to enter the kitchen. She stood in the doorway and spoke to Seamus. The early morning sunlight silhouetted her figure in the nightdress. She was not thin, but she wasn't large either. Let's say she was curvy, and I must admit that, at least as far as I was concerned, all of those curves were in the right places. She had what my mum would have termed 'child-bearing hips'. I suddenly felt a hot flush of shame in my admiration of her figure. Fiona looked back over her shoulder at me, smiled, and gave me a wink, "coming right up!" she said. Wasn't it illegal to flirt at this time of the morning? After what seemed to be a little amount of fussing and fiddling in the kitchen, she returned with what passed for a decent breakfast. As she sat down I could see that Fiona possessed what would be described in an old novel as an 'ample bosom' – definitely visible, but not overpowering. I pinched the bridge of my nose to wake myself up and, more importantly for me, to take my mind off the way it seemed to be heading.

We chatted over breakfast for a while, and then we decided we had to get ready to go out. Fiona made me promise that, while she was having a shower and getting ready, I should ring the hospital and get the 'news'. I had already realised that the one thing that you didn't do was not do what Fiona Mulgrew told you to do, so I did. Fiona returned a little later, wearing a dark green cable-knit sweater and denim skirt, drying her hair with a towel, hair which, as it was damp, seemed to have a deep, dark red chestnut colour.

"So, what news from the front, General?"

I explained that, as I feared, it did in fact appear that I had a malignant tumour attached to part of my pancreas, with additional small tumours on my liver. The hospital wanted me to start a course of chemotherapy in a week. The treatment would last four weeks, and I would be given a cocktail of chemicals that might make me feel quite ill.

"Still want to use me as your muse?"

"Too fecking right. You don't lose your inherent muse-ness with just one little bit of news!"

"Little bit of news?!" I sounded a little exasperated and not a little irritated.

"Trust me, Eeyore, we'll be fine. We'll get you through this little adventure together." As she said that, Fiona gave me an instinctive and reassuring nod. My irritability eased.

"Don't you want to hear the rest of the news?"

"What other news is there then? Oh, the prognosis!"

"The tumour is certainly at such an advanced stage as to make it inoperable. The chemo will shrink it, reduce it, slow it down, but it won't make it go away. It will never, ever go away and will kill me. Maybe not this week, or this month, but maybe this year and, if not, each year the odds get stacked against me even more. So it's likely 2012 will be my last year on this earth."

Fiona paused for thought for an instant, "so, how are we going to play this?"

"What do you mean?"

"Well, as far as I can see it there are four ways of dealing with this. Firstly, and most boringly, you could order your shroud now, turn up your toes and go and join the choir invisible. Apologies for the Monty Python quote; you aren't quite the Norwegian Blue, are you?"

I laughed, a deep hearty chuckle that cheered me instantly, which pleased Fiona no end, as obviously a fondness for Monty Python was something else we had in common, "or you could treat this as a wild festival of hedonism, living each day as if it's your last, sex drugs and rock 'n' roll a go-go, which might be fun. Option number three is to be fecking angry and fight each day, refusing to give up, which might well be the way to go. Finally you could enjoy days of abandon and adventure, doing what *you* want, and not what others expect of you, but wanting to wake up the next day. I know what I'd choose, but it's up to you. Either way, if it's still okay, I'd still like to do my sketches. Maybe you could keep a journal and we could produce a book at the end of it."

"Option number four sounds good to me. When do we start?" I asked, eagerly.

"After you have seen your kids, Eeyore, they have the utmost importance. They are far more significant than I am," Fiona sat beside me and held my head to the aforementioned ample bosom, which was pleasant to say the least, "and besides, I believe that children are the future…" At that we both burst out laughing, and then simultaneously ventured into a chorus of 'the Greatest Love of All'.

The drive from Eastbourne to Ticehurst, where my kids live with their mum and stepdad, took a little over an hour. It would have taken a little less, but for the need to let Seamus out to relieve himself just outside Battle. Ticehurst is a lovely little town in East Sussex. It's not one of these towns where supermarkets and town planners have destroyed its soul – it has traditional shops selling traditional goods, and not at over-inflated prices, either. Luckily for me the Easter holidays had begun a couple of days previously, and my ex had fairly willingly accepted my need to see the kids as a matter of urgency. Fortunately we had remained friends, as I feel that bearing grudges is one of the most pointless wastes of energy that anyone can indulge in. Whilst Fiona took a stroll with Seamus in the local park, I set off to do what felt like the hardest thing in the world to do, to tell the three people who I loved most in the world that their dear old dad was going to leave them one day in the not-so-distant future. I had asked Fiona to accompany me, but I realised that she was entirely correct that this was a task that I must do alone, not least as the kids had never met her and might wonder where I had encountered this Wicklow whirlwind who had entered my life only the day before.

Alex, the lady who once had taken the ludicrous decision to become Mrs Robbins, opened the door to me with a welcoming smile. The children had just nipped to the shop to buy some cakes, so I took the opportunity to ask her if I could have a word with her and her husband, James, with whom I enjoyed a cordial, if not blissful, acquaintance. We sat in the kitchen over a cup of coffee. It's only when I am coffee-deprived, which I had been due to Fiona's crockery accident, that I fully savour its deep, rich flavour and the hit of caffeine. Well, I would have been like that if Alex had ever been able to make coffee properly. Anyway, I explained what was going on, what I had been told, and what the outlook was. Al, I'd always called her Al, mainly because it infuriated my ex mother-in-law, got up out of her seat and gave me a hug. Not because she suddenly realised she still loved me, but because she was a friend, a friend with whom I was responsible for the creation of three young lives. She was happy for me to handle this in any way I wanted, and she promised to be around to pick up any pieces necessary while I underwent treatment and in the future.

"Excuse me if I sound too previous, but I'll never let them forget you, you know. You'll always be their dad," she said, with a tear in her eye. James put his arms around her shoulders, not in a 'back off, she's mine!' kind of way, but to comfort his wife. He nodded his head towards me, which I took to mean that he agreed with every word she had said. He wasn't a bad old stick, I suppose. True, he was so uptight that it would probably be impossible to slide the thinnest of cigarette papers between the cheeks of his arse, and he was from Essex (sorry, my south of the Thames prejudice, there), but in all the years Alex had been with him he had never tried to replace me as a father figure for the children.

I heard the front door open. I heard a general commotion in the hall, as the kids took off their coats and shoes. Then they hurried into the kitchen to greet their visitor.

'Hi dad!" said Ellen as she came in. She was tall, slim and had shoulder-length chestnut hair. She put her arms around me and gave me a kiss on the cheek. Peter said a cheery 'hello' and gave me a hug. Being the youngest, I think he sometimes felt as if he was in the shadow of his elder sisters. He was of medium height, with a thin face and short, light-brown hair.

"It's Mister Silly! Hello daddy!" Lizzy had always called me Mr Silly, as I think she was the only one who appreciated my daft sense of humour. She bounded over to me like an athletic wallaby and threw herself into my arms. I winced a little as the impact of my middle child's body on mine caught the scar from the laparoscopy, but that didn't matter as I was with my children. She gave me the biggest hug and kiss that I have ever had, and it was as much as I could do to stop myself from bursting into uncontrollable tears there and then. Al suggested that we all go into the lounge to sit in comfort, and told the children that I had to discuss something with them. Trouble was, I thought to myself, how could I? How could I do something which I knew would break my children's hearts, and mine along with them? As we went and sat down in the lounge I was still wondering how I could crack this case.

"Right, you three. First of all I have to apologise for not seeing you too much of late. As you know, 'chartered accountant' is code for international playboy," I gave them all a wink. Peter looked puzzled, Ellen groaned at yet another of my dodgy jokes, and Lizzy squealed with delight, commenting that Mr Silly was 'in the building', "now I have got some news for you, that isn't the best news that I could give. I need you all to listen carefully to everything I have to say, no interruptions allowed, and I will answer any questions you've got at the end, okay?"

The children nodded their assent, and so I began. I tried not to be too syrupy about it, yet I didn't want to just starkly tell them that I was dying. Actually, to be honest, I didn't give them all the facts, as I didn't feel I needed to, and the one thing I didn't want to do was end up watching my kids waiting for me to die, trying to notice every perceptible change that would mean I was headed downwards. I told them that I was ill, and that there was an illness in an organ just behind my stomach. It was likely to make me very ill as I had treatment, but that every day I would fight to get better so the children could see me. In the meantime I knew that their mum and James would look after and love them during the times that I was not around.

Ellen had tears in her eyes as she looked at me.

"Oh, dad. Is it cancer?" she whispered.

"Yes princess, yes it is." I whispered back to her, hoping that my two younger children would not catch on.

Ellen then got up and quietly left the room. I didn't stop her, nor would I want to as I had always believed that my children should be able to make reasoned choices. She didn't want to be upset in front of the other two, and for that I was grateful. I could hear Alex reassuring her in the kitchen. Then Peter chimed in.

"You're not going to die are you?"

"Peter, I'm going to spend every single day fighting to get better. Dying isn't on my agenda."

Peter looked reassured, partially at least.

"Mr Silly doesn't die – he laughs in the sight of death, and then pokes it in the eye and stamps on its foot!" Lizzy always did have a way with words. She got up out of her chair, walked over to me in a very assured manner, put her arms around my neck and carefully whispered into my ear, "Daddy, I'm doing Latin at school now, and all I can say is '*non illegitimi carborundum* '".

When I started driving home with Fiona after seeing the kids, Fiona decided to tackle my one truly antisocial habit head-on.

"Why do you smoke?"

"I don't know really. Put it down to teenage rebellion."

"You've been smoking a long time then?"

"Since I was twenty-five, I think."

"But…"

"I was a late developer." Fiona laughed just a little.

In a desperate attempt to change the subject, I asked Fiona what *non illegitimi carborundum* actually meant, as I had studied German at school, and Latin was all Greek to me (that didn't get a laugh either). She laughed and told me exactly what its most common translation is…

Don't let the bastards grind you down!

An interruption

Testing, testing. Fiona here! I won't be incorporating what I write into Peter's journal until the future, and I hope to God that he doesn't mind. I met Peter last Wednesday up at Beachy Head. I was walking my dog, Seamus, and he was lying down looking as if he wanted the world to just leave him alone. I never was one to follow instructions, so I got chatting to him. Since that day we have chatted, laughed, cried and he has already become a very dear friend.

I did my first sketch of Peter this weekend – we were at his house and he was sleeping on the sofa. I just sat there and got out my sketchbook – so drawing number one is of a grown man, fast asleep yet busily catching flies. And boy can he snore! I thought it was a heard of wild boar thundering through the room.

Peter started his chemo last Monday. We trundled off to the hospital and he got 'gowned up', as it were. So he had to take this mixture of chemicals. The concoction looked as if it had recently been extracted from someone's gall bladder, but he took it like a man, even if it did look as if he was going to throw up immediately afterwards. He seemed to cope with it in much better spirit than I ever could.

Anyway, it's now Wednesday evening and Peter is seriously unwell. I don't mean unwell as in dying, at least I hope not, but since this afternoon he has been seriously spewing his guts up. Apparently it's a side effect of his treatment, but it's not nice and I seriously regret saying I'd empty the bucket. The vomit is an acrid, grey liquid, or should I say semi-liquid, and it smells of TCP, or some other disgusting chemical concoction.

There were a couple of phone calls this afternoon, both of which I wasn't expecting. The first was from Peter's mother, Sheila. She seemed fairly pleasant and we spoke about how he was keeping – I think Peter told her about me last weekend when he told her about his illness, as she didn't seem too shocked to hear my voice. I know I haven't met her yet, but she did sound very pleasant. The last thing she said to me was that she wanted Peter to be happy, and hoped he'd find it with me! Not sure if she has the wrong idea about me – I didn't start chatting to him last week because I wanted to jump him, but I have become very fond of him in this short time. I must say he is like no man I have ever been out with, although this is not a romantic time at all. I am not sure how it is all going to pan out, but I am fond of Eeyore, and I do like that twinkle in his eye!

The second call was a bit of a shock, as it was from his ex-wife! She didn't know about me, so I had to introduce myself. It felt like I was undergoing a game of Twenty fecking Questions! Anyway, she knows about me now, that I am spending time with Peter because we enjoy each other's company and that's about it. Her final words to me were a bit stark, though. She warned me 'make sure he doesn't get hurt.' I am not sure if she just wanted to make sure I looked after him or was telling me she'd be ready to send the boys round to work me over with a few spiked baseball bats. I hope it's the former.

Sir Pukealot is stirring now, as I just heard a groan from the upstairs room, so I had best sign off. I am not sure how much I will write or how often I will write, so shall we just play it by ear, okay?

Le cancer, nul points!

It was Sunday, the first Sunday after my treatment began, but the second one I had spent with Fiona. The day before we had spent in the pub garden at the Queen's Head, chatting, laughing and smiling. Fiona sketched me twice, as far as I am aware, that afternoon. The first was when I was looking intently at the Guardian crossword – I've only been able to solve it once in my entire life, and know for a fact that it was the day before Ellen was born. I had all day to look at it with little else to do as Alex was in labour but absolutely bugger all was happening. At the end of that day I was ecstatic – not because there was a prospect of impending offspring, but because there was a completed cryptic crossword for the first time ever.

The second sketch was an action portrait of me. Well, when I say action, I was drinking a pint of Sussex Best, which is my idea of heaven, even if my alcohol tolerance levels are being severely tested by Malcolm. Oh yes, Malcolm! Well, I did some research on coping methods that might help me cope better psychologically and physically with my illness, and one particular one that I came across was *externalisation*. I didn't even know that was a word! Anyway, apparently if you regard the tumour as an external thing or person, and refer to it in such a manner it can help people cope with the stresses of their illness. Now at this stage I am willing to try most things if they give me the chance to prolong my life (there's nothing like an impending death sentence to make you want to embrace as many days as possible). Things that I would not consider include sticking syringes full of donkey urine into my arse, not that I have read that anywhere. And so Malcolm was 'born'. He is a weedy, nasty, spiteful little prat – all pointy nose and sneering gaze – no-one likes him and he's an ugly little bastard with nothing positive to contribute to my life!

I have been so rough this week. I have been throwing up so much that I thought my arse was going to come out through my mouth and I'd turn myself inside-out. Still, I started feeling brighter yesterday morning and this weekend has been better. You might have noticed that my attitude has changed. All I can say is this externalising nonsense must be having some effect, that and being in the company of Fiona. Not forgetting Seamus, of course. What can I say about her? I must admit I was a little narked when she spoke to me at Beachy Head, but I am glad she did. She's warm, witty, and most important of all knows her real ale!

Today was pleasant, but also a total mess. It wasn't messy due to illness, but simply due to my inability to think things out. After breakfast which, as we were at my house, did include coffee due to the existence of coffee mugs, we chatted for a while. I had been wondering how we could spend the day. I had put on a mellow piece of music, 'Woodstock' by Matthews Southern Comfort. Fiona and I both sat in my living room in my little house in Winchelsea Beach, put our heads back and let the music wash over us. Then, all of a sudden, I opened my eyes and raised my head.

"Let's go to France!"

"Ooh là là! What a cool idea. But how?"

"Oh, Neef," I'd taken to calling her Neef to counteract the 'Eeyore' effect,"'tis but a tiny, insignificant detail. Here we are in the south east. We drive past Rye, across Romney Marsh, past Hythe and Dymchurch, we avoid taking the wrong turn to visit the nuclear power station at Dungeness, up to Ashford, onto the M20 and Bob's your uncle we're in Dover"

"Actually Bob was my Aunt Flora's lover, short for Roberta, but that doesn't matter now. So, what do we need to take?"

"Just ourselves! We buy a ticket at Dover and we're in France in just over an hour."

"How often does the boat go? I get awfully seasick, you know!"

"Ah, you'll be fine, I promise"

We got a few things together and headed off in the Volvo across the open expanse of Romney Marsh towards the vast metropolis of Ashford (spot the irony) and then on to Dover. We had both got passports handy, but sadly for this adventure Seamus had to stay at home. We had left him a comfy bed and some music playing. I crossed my fingers that he would be content with a spot of the Dave Brubeck Quintet... At 11:30 we headed up the ramp, on to the enormous ship that was going to speed us the 22 miles over to Calais. We eschewed the warmth of the passenger lounge and sat out in the open, in the raw maritime chill, taking in the sea breezes and trying to smile.

Fiona loved it! She adored being able to see the famous White Cliffs of Dover (even if they were a shitty grey colour) disappear away from us , and soon the not-so-picturesque view of Calais docks were ahead of us. After disembarking we drove out of the port and parked up in the town centre. Very soon we were strolling along in the spring sunshine, looking at the array of ghastly and tacky souvenirs that were available in the various gift and souvenir shops.

Suddenly Neef's eyes were drawn to something shimmering in the window, something silver, simple and simply exquisite.

"Hey, Eeyore, will you take a look at that."

"What? The necklace?" It was a simple, yet stunning, piece of silver.

"Yeah, it's beautiful... just my style. Look at that price, though!"

"Yeah, have they put too many zeros on it? Hold on a second."

I walked into the shop and left Neef waiting, bemused, outside. She peered into the shop through the window but the lack of light inside, combined with the sunshine outside, made ascertaining what was going on a little more tricky than it normally would be. A few moments later I walked out of the shop and handed Fiona a small box.

"What's this?"

"It's a bloody nuclear reactor, isn't it? Open it, for God's sake!"

Fiona opened the box and found the necklace she had admired so much inside. She gazed at it in wonder, smiled, then looked at me.

"Oh Eeyore, it's even more beautiful in my hand than it was in the window... you shouldn't have... I mean, you shouldn't have!"

She passed the box back to me and walked away. I was utterly bemused. How easy was it to offend a woman, I thought. As she walked briskly up the street away from me, I was dumbfounded.

"Hey, Neef, hold on! Neef!" My voice grew steadily louder, "For God's sake, Neef, bloody well hang on. How bloody fast do you think a dying man can walk?"

Fiona stopped, turned on her heels, and walked straight back to me. When she finally stopped, I didn't have a chance to say anything.

"So why did you buy me this, why?"

"I..."

"I s'pose you think you have to buy me every single thing that I express even the slightest liking for, do you?"

"I..."

"I assume you think you have to buy my company so that you have someone to come on madcap daytrips with, do you?"

"I... it's nothing like that at all. I l...like you, and I wanted to buy it for you."

"You like me? Is that all?"

"Let's not go there, Neef. I just wanted to buy you it, nothing more, nothing less."

Fiona's frown changed into a smile.

"You stupid daft bastard, there's no need. I'm sorry for going off on one at you... it's just I am not used to receiving gifts like this. Paul, my ex, was never one for buying me impromptu presents. Too busy up to his spit-valve in some tart from London, I guess. I am really sorry."

"There's nothing to apologise for, nothing at all. Lunch?"

"What a sensible chap you are, Eeyore."

We made our way back to the car and drove to a little restaurant that I knew just outside Dunkerque. A delicious chicken lunch accompanied by a bottle of Perrier was in order for me, as I was driving and didn't want to upset my stomach with too much rich food and drink. Fiona decided not to join me in my celebration of temperance and had a cheeky little Malbec with her steak-frites. Over coffee we chatted - long serious topics and absolute crap, often simultaneously – and then headed back to the car.

"Eeyore, I have absolutely loved today" she said as we sat atop the ferry once again on our way back to Dover, "I love your lifestyle, your house, and everything we have done thus far." I saw such a glorious sparkle in her eyes.

Her necklace sparked on her neck in the afternoon sunlight. Fiona smiled at me.

"I've never been to France before."

"There are nicer places than bloody Calais, I can tell you."

"It doesn't matter; it's the company that is important. You really are a lovely man."

Over Fiona's shoulder I caught a glimpse of a couple kissing on deck, and so very much in love. I looked at Fiona once more, and looked intensely at her smiling face. There was warmth, tenderness and companionship. I thought I saw a glint of something else, and so lowered my head towards hers. She tilted her head slightly so that there would be no unnecessary clashing of noses when our lips finally met and, to my mind at least, hopefully never left each other. This would be the perfect end to the day, I thought. It wouldn't be the end, though, as we still had the evening!

All of a sudden I caught a waft of the garlic mayonnaise and red wine that Fiona had consumed and, as a result of my illness I later maintained, as I am not at all averse to either, I was hit by such a sudden wave of nausea that I barely reached the side of the ship than I suddenly began vomiting as if, funnily enough, my life depended on it. Every single part of my calorific intake on this beautiful day, croissants, chicken, potatoes, mineral water and coffee, not forgetting the little biscuit that accompanied my café au lait, took this once in a lifetime opportunity to exit my digestive tract via the nearest available emergency exit. It didn't stop to pick up its luggage, or to dawdle chatting to its neighbours, and I can tell you I felt absolutely wretched. Not only was I expecting a kitchen sink to exit my mouth in this vomit jamboree, but I had also totally ballsed up my first potentially romantic moment in years. How on earth was Neef going to want to kiss me if my lips tasted of regurgitated foodstuffs?

Fiona walked up behind me and started rubbing my back in a comforting manner. She hugged me and gave my shoulder a kiss.

"Oh, Eeyore, you are a poorly boy, aren't you?" She carried on holding me until we reached the mainland. When we got back into the car, for what would prove to be a car journey interspersed with brief 'spew stops' in lay-bys, she squeezed my thigh and said "the moment is not gone, merely resting."

Ooh là là (Fiona's Log)

What a fabulous day! I cannot say what a wonderful time I am having with Peter. Today, he suddenly decided that we should visit France, basically just for lunch. I have never been there before, and I was really worried that I would be seasick like I used to be on the boat from Fishguard to Rosslare, but no. Eeyore also bought me a wonderful necklace. It was so sweet of him, even if I seemed ungrateful at first.

I am not sure what happened on the way back. Well, I know that Eeyore was violently sick for most of the ferry crossing – and he said he never gets seasick! My arse! I couldn't tell him I thought he was all mouth and trousers before the trip, as his ego is still a little fragile. It is probably a lot fragile after what I intend to term 'the moment'. I had consumed such a wonderful lunch, with perfect company, and I was maybe a little squiffy from the red wine I'd been drinking.

On the drive back from Dover to Winchelsea Beach, my mind was a whirl. After about an hour I couldn't concentrate properly on the road ahead, so I pulled into a lay-by, left the sleeping Eeyore in the passenger seat, picked up his cigarettes and went outside for a smoke. This would have been absolutely fine were it not for the fact that I have never smoked before in my whole life.

After a while, Peter awoke and got out of the car. He found me sitting on the warm bonnet of the Volvo, puffing away on a particularly noxious cigarette in a panicky fashion.

"Neef, what's wrong?"

I stubbed out the barely smoked cigarette, leaving it a smouldering remnant on the ground at my feet.

"Why do you smoke these fecking things? I'm okay, just taking a break. You get back in the car and rest, 'kay?"

Peter was acutely aware about my edginess, not that I was trying to hide it.

"What's happened?"

"Nothing, nothing's happened. I'm just... just a little mixed up."

"Mixed up about what?"

"Well, if I knew the answer to that I wouldn't be so fecking confused, would I? Look, I'm sorry, I just... I just need to work out in my head where all this is headed."

"What's this?"

"You don't know?"

"Well, I could guess."

"Then you'd probably guess right."

"Look, I don't know either. They do say, though, that a straight line may be the shortest distance between two points, but it's by no means the most interesting."

"Where'd you pick up that gem?"

"Doctor Who, 1973"

"You really are a mine of useless information, aren't you, Eeyore?" I smiled at him apologetically. We got into the car and headed off back to Winchelsea Beach.

As I've said before, I had never even considered Peter as a potential romantic interest, but it seemed just right that we'd kiss. He may be a little chunky, and a little bald, but he has such a beautiful outlook on life.

And I am worried. I am frightened that I am falling for him, for the man with the blue sick bucket. If I continue falling for him, what happens at the end? How can I continue if I give my heart to a man who I know is going to die, just as we should both be enjoying each other's company, and savouring each other in other ways as much as we can?

Oh shit, I am so mixed up at the moment. I can feel myself physically wanting him. I think I have fallen in lust with him, but what is going to happen if I fall in love? I've only ever really been in love once before in my life, and he ended up sleeping with the brass section of the Notting Hill Symphonia. Now I am contemplating giving my heart to a man who is going to bugger off and die, literally!

It's all such a fecking mess. I am such a mess in my head. What on earth should I do? We're back at hospital tomorrow and then he'll be ill again, and I will have to sit there turning over in my mind how this is going to pan out. It would be so much easier if we could get the messy business of sex out of the way, but I suppose that will have to wait. But I can't wait! Oops, *in vino veritas* as they say in Dundalk. I must admit I am sitting here wondering about many things. Should we even try to make a go of it? Should I jump him and take him by surprise? And what if the dog joins in?

I hope I find the answer soon. I need to get back to Eastbourne, back on home turf. That might help. I hope to God that it does.

Isn't that a small one!

I haven't been up to writing much over the last few weeks. The continued doses of my usual chemical cocktail have taken their toll, and I haven't been up to doing much. This is, therefore, a catch-up report.

Week two saw only a day of throwing up, a series of light lunches, and on Saturday I endured a 'familial visit'. My mum came down to see me along with Alice, my elder sister, her prat of a husband, Norman, and their children, Rhoda and Cecily. I suppose I mustn't grumble, and it was actually quite nice seeing them, but they don't half bloody fuss! It was all 'are you eating well?' this, and 'have you taken your vitamins?' that, and I was waiting for 'can you remember how to wipe your arse?' Mum did the thing that annoys me the most – she came in and she tidied up! I didn't ask her to and I wasn't in the mood to. Let's face it; I am as happy as a pig in muck if I am living like a pig in muck.

So now I was in a house that gleamed as if it had just been silver-plated and placed in a display cabinet. I was now an exhibit on display, an invalid who looks as if he is able, and by inference willing, to 'receive visitors'. I will state categorically right now that I am seldom willing to receive visitors, even when I am not dying.

And so they all sat down with a pot of tea and all the accompanying paraphernalia and tried to make conversation. We discussed the weather, and all wondered whether it was going to turn to Spring soon, my hopes for the prospects of Kent County Cricket Club this upcoming season (I just about refrained from saying my hope was that I'd live to see the end of the season), and then Alice decided to overload the crass-ometer.

"So, Peter, what's all this about a lady friend, then? I must say you are a dark horse!" At this I wish I had the theme tune to Black Beauty lined up on the CD player, but my gift for natural comedy is lacking, as you may well be aware reading this already.

"Where is this Fiona today?"

"*This* Fiona? Have I been out with a whole production line of Fionas? I am sorry, sis, she escaped off her leash just as I was washing her down for presentation, hoping she'd get 'Best in Show'."

"Well, there's no need to be like that!"

"Well… Look, I'm sorry, sis, it's the cancer talking. Can I take back that last diatribe?" I sighed. "Truth is, Fiona is having a weekend at home, washing and catching up on the million and one things she has neglected since she met me and decided to study me."

"Study you?" Alice and Norman looked at one another, slightly puzzled.

I then explained the circumstances of the meeting of Fiona and I, how we had chatted and enjoyed each other's company, and how Fiona had asked to do a number of portraits of me. After protestations and comments from all the family, supposedly out of concern for my welfare, I managed to placate them and explain that I was 'merely' suffering from cancer, and hadn't yet taken the drastic step of having my brain removed. They left that evening with just a little more understanding, I suppose due to tolerance for the fact that this member of the family was going to die; they tried their best to understand, even if they didn't actually do so.

The following week was dull and full of chemicals and radiotherapy, but at the end of the week Alex and James brought the children over to see me. There was no need to stand on ceremony. They promised that they would sort out food in the kitchen and leave me to have time with Ellen, Lizzy and Peter. We played Scrabble, I pulled silly faces, I was given loads of cuddles (they are on prescription, you know), and I had a fantastic day, and the smile didn't disappear from my face for a long time.

Before you ask, yes, Fiona was there. She met the children, and Alex and James. As far as the kids were concerned she was a friend of mine who was staying; they didn't bat an eyelid, apart from Lizzy, who gave me a cheeky wink when no-one else was looking, telling me to behave myself. And they all absolutely loved Seamus, who was such a tart in accepting all this new-found affection.

God, this feels like an episode of 'The Two Ronnies'. And in a packed programme tonight, there are two other pieces of news. Firstly, my pension company finally coughed up and paid out. I suppose there are some benefits to being terminally ill. I now have a decent amount of money to live on, or should I say, die on. With that, and mortgage insurance paying it off, I am now in a position to enjoy my death. That sounds so morbid - I think black humour is my 'thing' nowadays.

I was going to leave it, all my money etc. to the kids, but they don't mind, at least Al and James told me they don't. Sure, I will leave them something, but it's not as if they are living hand to mouth in Ticehurst, as James has a successful business, and they haven't got any children of their own together. Al and James told me that they wanted me to enjoy my final days, as it were, and to concentrate on being happy.

The second news item should deserve a chapter of its own, but I am so delighted I can hardly bear the excitement. After this week's treatment, I was asked if I'd pop down and slip myself into the microwave in the CT Scanner Room, because they were all eager to know how long it would take to cook me at 180 degrees so that I would be tender and ready for Christmas dinner. Well, after looking at my scans, and avoiding my comment of 'how do you want me, Mr de Mille?', the head honcho in the scanner room, who worryingly always wore rubber gloves, walked over to have a word. It suddenly occurred to me that he might be a proctologist on a sabbatical, but who still wanted to keep his hand in, as it were. My sphincters instinctively tightened.

Mr Sadiq, who actually was a Oncology specialist, and not a proctologist or, thankfully, a jobbing window cleaner looking to supplement his income, was delighted to show me that my primary tumour had shrunk to the size of an anorexic walnut as a result of my chemotherapy. I asked what this meant in terms of my prognosis, and was slightly shocked to hear that, at the moment, there was no change to that. It didn't matter that it had shrunk; the important thing was that it stayed as shrunken for as long as possible. The average prognosis was that I had four to six months, but that anything beyond that was pure guesswork. Still, at the moment, I was happy to accept those odds. He did, though, point out to me that long-term survival rates for pancreatic cancer hadn't changed in forty years, and with my relatively late diagnosis, it wasn't likely at all to have a happy ending.

Icing on the cake?

You may have noticed that these journal entries don't have a day entry on them. It's a bit like Christmas, but instead of a jolly fat man in a red suit with a white beard causing me to forget what day it was, this time it's the Grim reaper himself. As I was getting confused, I decided to go through my journal up to now and delete them all.

I couldn't wait to share the news with anyone who dared to allow me the chance to bore them. I think I even kissed Mr Sadiq. Anyway, that evening, I drove over to Neef's so we could have a bite to eat, and enjoy a few glasses of beer.

I decided we should dine out, so we strolled off to The Lamb and had a delicious meal. I opted for the snail fricassee followed by a lamb shank, and Neef opted for squid as a starter and roast pork. My! How the Sussex Best flowed that evening! Fiona was as delighted as I to hear my news from the hospital and, though she also knew that I was still living under a death sentence, we both hoped that my stay of execution would last as long as possible. We wobbled up the hill to Neef's flat and staggered in laughing and giggling. I had bought her some new coffee mugs, so we were able to have a sobering cuppa as we sat and chatted.

"Neef, I am so happy today, I need to wake up now and live!"

"Oh Eeyore, I am so pleased for you. You can now hopefully see your kids grow up a little more, as well as endure more of your mum tidying up after you!"

"Yes, thank you for that," I yawned, "I'm sorry, I have landed on planet Shattered. D'you mind?"

"It's no worry at all. We've got tomorrow, and the day after that and after that etc…" She leant over and kissed me on the forehead, "I really am so happy for you. Night!"

She got up, and left the room to allow me to get to sleep. Seamus followed after her, as he had found that Fiona's bed was just as comfortable as the sofa I had wrested from his grasp. I finished the final slurp of my coffee, sleepily pulled off my shirt and trousers, and settled down to sleep.

I am not sure how long I had been asleep, but in the darkness of the wee small hours I woke to hear footsteps in the corridor outside the lounge. The door opened and Fiona entered the room.

"What's wrong?" I whispered, just about realising where I was and who it was who was interrupting my sleep.

"Sshh… nothing's wrong, nothing's wrong in the slightest. I wanted to come and see you, to um... oh feck it!"

"Why did you want to see me?"

"Can't you guess?"

"Well, I could, but I worry I might offend you."

"How about I give you a clue."

She stood by the sofa, crossed her arms and took hold of the sides of the nightdress, raising it up and pulling it over her head, revealing to me at long last, I thought, her beautifully curvy shape, which excited me greatly as I saw it in the gloom.

"You like?" She whispered. I was genuinely speechless. I nodded, then nodded more eagerly, and moved over to make a space for her under the duvet. My body was stirring in ways that it hadn't stirred in years. Fiona slipped in beside me on my makeshift bed, and I took her in my arms. Her skin was milky white and soft to the touch, with no blemishes as far as I could make out in the limited light. I leant over her and kissed her full on the lips. I am still too much of a gentleman to go into great detail here, but things did progress, slowly but surely, then more firmly and pressingly, leading to a great deal of mutual happiness.

My biggest fear that night was whether this was real, or just a wonderful wish-fulfillment dream. I kissed Fiona on the nose. She giggled and snuggled down into my chest and gently fell asleep. I then realised that I should get some sleep too. I would find out if it had been a dream when I woke up. If I had company, I'd be in rapture. If alone, I'd know it had merely been wish-fulfillment. I settled down to a night of impatient slumber, hopefully with the stunningly sexy Fiona in my arms.

I slept for what seemed like hours. As my eyes became accustomed to the hints of daylight straining their way through a minute gap in the curtains, I initially forgot what I was hoping to find when I awoke properly. I was bunched up against the back of the sofa, but there was no woman in my arms. I thought for a moment about my disappointment, and tried to be rational. I had had a fantastic dream, I thought, but it would be unfair on Fiona for me to undertake a relationship with her, a relationship in the full-blown physical, sexual sense, I mean. What would it lead to anyway? Sure, we would make love as if our lives depended on it, but eventually she'd end up being involved with an older man who she'd see wither away and die in front of her, just as she'd (hopefully) be falling more and more for him. Could I bear for that to happen? Could I be that cruel? I certainly didn't regard myself as the last of the red-hot lovers, or even the lukewarm ones, the kind of man who would spoil Neef and make it impossible for her to contemplate a physical liaison with another man after me, but it would be the most hurtful thing I had done, I thought to myself, to allow someone to fall in love with me and, by consequence, cause her the most god-awful grief and sense of loss when I died. No, it was probably best that it was this way, as I thought too much of Fiona to hurt her like that when my premature death was the only sure-fire outcome in this life.

I playfully slapped myself on the cheek, shook my head, and dozed off for some more rest.

Over-thinking

I woke for a second time at around ten o'clock. The sound that brought me to my senses was Fiona entering the flat, stumbling over the threshold with a carrier bag full of sundry items that I could not make out through the semi-transparent plastic.

"Morning!" Fiona was certainly in a bright and breezy mood, and I decided not to discuss with her had gone through my mind earlier, and certainly not what I had dreamed the night before. "I hope I didn't wake you earlier. I could see you were sleeping so soundly that it would be rude to wake you."

She put down the carrier bag, reached over me and kissed me on the forehead. "How are you this fine morning?"

"Well, to be honest my mind has been whirring. Don't ask me what, as it would be too hard to describe." I would have continued chatting, but I was bemused by Fiona kicking off her shoes and immediately divesting herself of her jumper, skirt and socks!

"Ta-da! How do you like me in the daylight then? I tell you what, Eeyore, your tail certainly wagged last night!" She gave me the cheekiest wink ever.

"Shall I give you a twirl?" She spun round. I was speechless. I spluttered and tried to utter a coherent sound, but was taken aback when she started taking off her bra and knickers. She stood naked beside me for an instant then positively leapt under the covers with me once again. She put her arm around me, gave me the deepest kiss on the lips.

"Mmmm, you certainly know how to show a girl a good time! I hope you weren't shocked that I wasn't here earlier, but I had to nip off to the chemist. You see, it's been such a long time since I slept with anyone that had completely forgotten about contraception. Yes, I know, a good catholic girl like me shouldn't know about these things, but I was also in the scouts! You have to be prepared and, if not, you need to nip to the chemist the next day! Oh my lord I am talking forty-six to the dozen, aren't I? But I tell you what; I don't fecking care, even if my hips ache a little this morning!"

I was still lost for words. I looked intently at Neef. I drank in the features of the woman who had woken up my spirit a few weeks before, and who had brought physicality back to my life a few short hours before. I smiled, or at least tried to. Don't get me wrong, being given a seeing-to by a woman fifteen years my junior had done wonders for my self-esteem, but the concerns that I had thought about earlier, hadn't disappeared, had they? Wasn't I being the biggest shit in existence by allowing this to happen? Could I be this unfair to Fiona, a woman with whom I obviously shared a physical attraction, and for whom my feelings obviously ran as deep as the Bakerloo Line?

"Neef, we have to talk."

"Of course we do! How else will I be able to tell you what I want you to do to me?" She smiled.

"No, I mean we *really* need to talk! If this is going to happen, how is it going to end? We both know I am under a death sentence. It can't be fair on you for me to start a physical relationship with you. I'm not saying that I regret last night, but I am uneasy. Does that make sense?"

"Sure it does, Eeyore. That's one of the things I love about you..." she paused for a second, and I wasn't quite sure why, "feck, did I just fecking say I fecking loved you? That's a bit of a leap in the dark, a bit like us two last night, I guess." She had a real giggle in her voice this morning!

"You... love me?"

"Aye, I guess I do. Isn't that weird? Or isn't it? Or does it matter at all? How's about you, then, Eeyore? How do you feel?"

I was sorely tempted to say I felt horny, but I tried once more to deal with what is all too often called the 'elephant in the room'.

"But what about my illness?"

"Malcolm? Well sure, but he's not going to get anywhere near giving me a seeing-to!"

"Be serious now."

"Look. Who gives a feck about your cancer? Stop worrying about what others think, or what is going to happen in the future. It's quite simple – I have fallen head over heels for you. I am smitten with you. You've made me feel in a way that I haven't felt in ages, years even. Sure, if I were to be brutally honest I started fancying you when I saw you looking at me in my nightie after the first night you stayed over." I thought that I was a plain-speaker, but Neef's frankness about relationships made be blush a little.

"Have I embarrassed you, you darling little fecker? I don't know how clearly I can put this to you. I am yours; I'm giving myself to you! I am saying that I am prepared to put up with the sadness then, in return for the happiness now. I s'pose that's part of the bargain I am making with myself now, in return for happiness with a man I care so very deeply about," she stroked the line of my eyebrow, "and hopefully nights like the one I had last night!"

Fiona kissed me full on the lips and lifted herself on top of me. I placed my hands on her buttocks and pulled them closer to me. This was going to be one hell of a journey!

Part Two – The Now

Officialdom

I hate rollercoasters. Scrub that, I love rollercoasters. No, I hate them. Oh shit, this is confusing. When I am at a theme park I stand nervously in the line, waiting to get on to the white-knuckle ride. Then I get to the cars, the safety bar comes down and the ride starts. It goes along a bit and then up, and up and up, and by this stage I am normally bricking myself. By the time the cars reach the top of the chained lift and you are about to drop, well, it's a surprise they don't paint the cars of all rollercoasters brown. And then the whoosh starts. Sweeping down, and up, and round, and looping the loop, and up again, for yet more! Throughout this I am breathing deeply and trying to look stony-faced, willing myself to get through to the end without suffering a cardiac arrest. And then, finally, the ride reaches the end, I gingerly get up out of the car, walk out of the exit and exclaim triumphantly 'shit, wasn't that great!' And the worst thing is, I mean every single word.

That last paragraph pretty much sums up how I feel at the moment. I adore being with Neef. To be able to enjoy her company, her wit, her sparkling conversation, and everything else besides.

And then I think of Neef. I must admit I like thinking of her. Just being in her company lights up a room. I cannot imagine life without her. I cannot imagine what will happen when my life ends. I know I am very seriously ill, but I think I can sum it up like this. Fiona is not a woman I can live with; she's a woman I cannot live without.

Shit! I guess that means... I love her! You love her, you bloody idiot. Now tell her, for Christ's sake.

So that's what I did. I got up out of the sofa. Note there I said 'out of' as I was still struggling with its lack of springs. I walked gingerly to Fiona's bedroom, as it was still virgin territory for me. She had just been having a shower and, I guessed, was getting ready for the day ahead. The door was open. I walked in, and sat on the bed. Moments later Neef walked into the room, wrapped in a turquoise bath towel.

"To what do I owe this pleasure, Eeyore?" she asked, with a smile.

"Oh Neef, did you mean what you said? I mean, about ignoring my illness, and being willing to put up with it and loving me?"

"I wouldn't say so if I didn't mean it."

"Well, that is very pleasing, because, I have been thinking... and..."

"Fecking well get on with it!" There was no anger in her voice, she was smiling broadly, and adjusting the top of her towel with her left hand. She then picked up her glasses from the dressing table.

"Well, I sat there while you were in the shower, and I realised that I am nothing without you in my life. Quite simply... I realised I love you, too."

Fiona squealed with delight and pulled off her towel. She stood there, her body glistening wet like an overgrown sea lion, and then leapt on top of me, kissing me as if she hadn't done so in weeks.

"Eeyore, I am so happy. Let's make plans. How are we going to spend the time we have left?"

"I have one more question"

"And what would that be? You aren't going to take advantage of me while I'm in the nip, are you?"

"Well, that might be in order, but I am one for doing these things properly, especially as I am going to die one day fairly soon. I want to make things official, so that you are provided for when I am gone..."

"Don't talk about things like that, I don't fecking want to think about life when you're gone, not now, not after you've just told me you love me."

"I realise that, and maybe I am phrasing it wrong. Classic overthinking yet again. Look, I'll put it simply..."

"I fecking well wish you would!" Fiona was toying with me, I could sense.

"Neef, will you do me the honour of becoming my wife?"

"Oh, Eeyore! Yes... YES!" She launched herself upon me once again, wrapping her legs around the back of mine, gripping me ever so tightly, and showing how much my question had delighted her. "Let's do it soon! I can't wait to become Mrs Peter Robbins. Wait a sec, you promise you won't go off and start shagging a trombonist?"

"Of course not! I do know the accordion player from the Lewes Ceilidh band, though."

"You silly fecker!" Fiona started kissing me and I realised that I could now start living my life again, a life that had been on hiatus for far too long. I also realised that we'd probably have to have a shower again a bit later.

Mr & Mrs Silly

I couldn't wait to tell the world, but I must admit, impressing people or, more importantly, surprising people, is so bloody difficult. After celebrating our sudden engagement by, both of us together, cuddling Seamus to within an inch of his life, I realised that I should tell people about the decision that Neef and I had taken together. I was so, so ecstatic that I was to spend the little time remaining in the company of such a wonderful woman. The first person I thought I had best tell was mum, which also had some hidden benefits, as she would break out the familial jungle drums and pretty soon everyone would know, and I could save on my phone bill. How do you think the news of my illness spread so rapidly?

Mum was cagey about it. I suppose there is a little bit of shock due when you find out that your son is planning to marry the woman who he has met only a few weeks beforehand. But who cares, if she can't be happy for me then that's her lookout, not mine!

I had to tell the kids, and decided that Neef and I would tell them together, when they came over to mine the following weekend. The kids loved her already. Ellen respected her as someone who made me happy, which made her happy. Peter just liked her, as he never really let people know what was going on inside his head, which worried me a touch. Because he was so guarded, I just knew in my heart of hearts that it would hit him like the proverbial brick wall when I finally did leave him and all those others whom I held so dear. Lizzy had found a kindred spirit in Fiona. They shared the same kind of madcap lunacy, always looking for the absurd rather than the mundane. Would they all manage to rub along properly after I was gone? I mean, I knew they all got on, but Fiona was more of an age that she could be a big sister, rather than their step mum. That, I reasoned, I would have to leave to chance, and to trust in their judgment, as when it came about I wouldn't be able to do much about it.

When Saturday came, we decided to push the boat out. Now I am not averse to rustling up the odd slap-up meal, or hearty roast dinner, which was handy as Neef's culinary skills were more cordon d'off than cordon bleu. On this occasion, though, we went to the fish and chip shop to dine, or to purchase, as Lizzy so eloquently put it, 'Ambrosia from far-off Rye Harbour', along with a bottle of 'Chateau Sarsons'. It was a shame she had never met my dad but, then again, she'd have been effing and blinding her way through middle school.

When the time finally arrived for me to tell the children, there was a genuine reaction of shock. Peter gave me a gentle hug, and then gently kissed Fiona on the cheek. Lizzy rose like a salmon out of her seat and cried out 'Mr and Mrs Silly!' She ran to Fiona and hugged her as if her life depended on it, then leapt over to me and kissed me, saying 'you have chosen well, young Jedi!' What was I going to do with her? The final one was the one I was more than a little worried about. Ellen and I had always had a close, yet quiet relationship. She wasn't one for grand, extravagant gestures of affection or big, open, heart-to-heart conversations. I could see that my big girl, as I always referred to her, had a tear in her eye yet again.

"Oh, dad!"

"What's wrong, princess?"

Ellen walked towards the kitchen door.

"I hope you're okay with this, Ellen."

"What if I'm not?"

"Well, it's going to happen whether you like it or not."

Fiona decided to chime in at this point and, to be honest, she was right.

"Eeyore, shut up. Ellen, I know you and your daddy are close, very close in fact. And it's stressful at a time when he's so ill, let alone with a newcomer on the scene, eh?'

Ellen's eyes didn't rise from the floor.

"Something like that, I s'pose"

"Look, I understand, and let me say that I don't want to come between you and your daddy."

"Well, I'd only want to go ahead if everyone were happy."

"Well, it's not a case of happy, I guess. Let me rephrase this, if I can. Dad, Fiona, are you both absolutely sure this is what you want to do?"

I was taken aback.

"I wasn't expecting to be questioned by my eldest daughter, but yes, I am."

"So am I, Ellen. I love your daddy so much, and it would mean a lot to me to have your approval."

Ellen was really on the verge of a full-blown blub, but she walked calmly over to me and threw her arms around me. I thought she would never let me go, but I was amazed when she outstretched one of her arms and brought Fiona into the hug! I think we were all teary at the end of it, although Peter maintained he had something in his eye. That's my boy!

I'd forgotten how much planning and organising weddings require. I also had to go through the trial of meeting Fiona's relatives. Her parents had died a few years back, and she was an only child, but I did get to meet her uncle Dermot who, it transpired, called her Fifi – always had done so, always would.

"If you just so much as call me fecking Fifi once, I'll fecking finish you off!" she warned me with a smile.

We were neither of us overly religious, and so we chose to get married at the very picturesque David Salomons' House on the outskirts of Tunbridge Wells. Sir David Salomons was a famous figure in Victorian society. He served as Lord Mayor of London and was also one of the very first Jewish people to serve in the House of Commons. He was also England's first Jewish magistrate. Broomhill, his house, is located in stunning parkland not far from the small town of Southborough. I remembered it from my childhood. It was designed in the 1830s by Decimus Burton, and is set in glorious grounds. The house features many features, including a water tower, stables, laboratories and a theatre, featuring its own organ.

I chose to wear a dark grey lounge suit with a pair of Mr Silly socks (I couldn't resist), and Peter joined me as my best 'man', dressed in a similar style, but in a much smaller size of course. Ellen wore a jacket and skirt, while Lizzy wore a floaty summer dress in a gorgeous Laura Ashley-style pattern. Mum wore a big hat. She always wore a big hat. Don't get me wrong, she wasn't stark naked apart from the hat, but the hat always got gasps from the audience. I asked her if she wanted me to take her to Mexico so she could fall asleep next to a city wall and, even though I am forty-four years old, she threatened me with a smacked arse! Don't you just love mothers? Seamus was there, being as quiet and obedient as ever, as were the rest of my family, obedient or otherwise. All participants in the ceremony, and all the guests, wore purple ribbons as a sign of solidarity for awareness of my illness.

So what of my best girl? By tradition I had no idea whatsoever what Fiona was going to wear. I was blown away by her when she did appear. She wore a crimson evening gown, quite simply styled, but with a slit up the left hand side that gave me a tantalising glimpse of her leg as she walked towards me. I was allowed to sit, due to my illness, but I forced myself to stand when she reached the registrar's table.

We had taken some time over deciding our vows. We had decided that Fiona should go first.

"Peter, I must admit that I had not set out this year to find myself a husband, but I am so pleased to have found you. I know full well that the days we have had have, thus far not been the easiest, but they have been joyous, as I have been with you. The days we have ahead of us will certainly not be easy either, but we *will* make them joyous. I will treasure every memory of every day I am with you, and will love you until the day I die. I will treasure and honour your memory, and keep your memories alive for my stepchildren, now, always, and forever."

Most of the congregation was now in floods of tears. How could I follow that?

"My darling Fiona, until this year I was a happy divorcee, spending my life working or being with my children or family. I hadn't thought about being in need of a wife, but then you came along, and you have brightened up this very dark period of my life. Who knows how much longer it will last, but we will make the most of every single one. I will not tell you if I am marrying you just to become a dog owner, but let's just say that Seamus is a welcome addition. I know that my whole family adore you, especially the children, and they have never seen me so happy. I will continue to love, adore and cherish you until the day I am gone. And even then I may choose to come back and haunt you just to be in your company!"

Fiona had tears in her eyes now. She quietly whispered 'I love you Eeyore!' and kissed me, just as the registrar indicated that such a thing was in order.

Malcolm, don't you dare balls up my life! Here I was, properly in love for the first time in ages. I held Fiona in my arms as the congregation applauded, Mum was dabbing at her eyes with a hanky, Alice and Norman and the kids were hugging. Even my little brother Adam was there, standing around literally like a spare part at a wedding, with his pompous German girlfriend Claudia at his side, who had a look of total disinterest in the whole event. Alex and James hugged, Auntie Maud just applauded. I beckoned to the kids and they came and joined in with Fiona and myself. One huge hug, one enormous expression of joy during a very dark time for me. Even Seamus came and jumped up and joined in the group hug, standing on his hind legs with his front paws on the lot of us.

The evening reception was brilliant. There was music, dancing and singing. There was much love and affection in evidence. Speeches were made, which were funny and poignant, even at the same time. Peter made a very good best man's speech, even at his young age. He spoke of his love for me and his sisters, and also of his new-found love for his new step mum, with whom he hoped to have a fantastic relationship throughout the future. I fought hard to fight back the tears as he spoke. I was so proud of him, proud of Lizzy and also proud of Ellen. It's only when you know you will lose something in the future that you cherish it while you have the chance.

As the time came for Fiona and me to depart, I whispered in her ear.

"I suppose you'd like to see your wedding present, then?"

"I thought we weren't? Eeyore, what the feck have you been up to?"

I tried my hardest to maintain an air of dotty aloofness. After I completed my treatment, both Neef and I had talked of doing a roadtrip of some description – travelling around the country and stopping off at places as the fancy took us. We walked out to depart the reception and start our honeymoon, and Fiona was astonished to see that my car, my trusty Volvo S80 was not there. In its place was a dark red Volkswagen camper van – very 1970s retro with the spare wheel in a hard cover on the front. This had been very tough to keep as a secret. Fiona looked at me, then at the van, then back at me. She gave a squeal of delight and flung her arms around me. This was to be our travelling companion for the trip. It was kitted out for everything we needed, and we could sleep in it if we wanted, but I had also asked my family and friends for recommendations for places to stay in different places as we travelled. Our journey could be leisurely, with no pressure, which was exactly what we wanted.

The only fixed destination, though, was where we were to spend our wedding night! We climbed into the van, I turned the key and we set off! Alex and James agreed to dog-sit Seamus for the night, which confused Fiona. We sped off in the van, and down the country lane that led from David Salomons' House. I didn't turn back up towards Tunbridge Wells, but instead drove down through some very pleasant villages – Speldhurst, Langton Green, Groombridge, Withyham, Hartfield, Wych Cross and eventually we reached the lovely, scenic country house hotel that I had selected in the middle of Ashdown Forest. Naturally I had booked the Bridal Suite. We checked in, and were taken to our room, where a large suite of rooms was opened up to us. Just as I requested a bottle of chilled champagne accompanied by, quite surprisingly, four bottles of Harveys Blue Label Bitter, awaited us in the room.

The door closed, and eventually Neef and I were finally alone. I was utterly exhausted, and in not a little pain. Still, I tried to hide that from Fiona, but her 'Malcolm sensors' were well-tuned.

"Well, Mrs Robbins, all I can say is thank you for becoming my wife."

"My darling Mr Robbins, it is quite simply my pleasure. Now you will be tired, and we need to get you off your feet and on your back." Fiona gently pushed me towards the bed, giggling. I lay down, thankful for the chance to be off my feet.

Fiona expertly opened the bottle of champagne and poured two glasses. She then came back into the bedroom and placed them on the bedside table.

"I think we'll pause here, don't you think?" Fiona climbed on to the bed, sliding her body across mine. She kissed me on the lips. "Close your eyes; it's time for your present!"

If it's Monday, it must be Dorset, or must it?

The next morning I woke to the sound of the birds in the trees, the smell of a room-service breakfast, and the sight of the new Mrs Peter Robbins lying in my arms, nuzzled against my chest. I gently kissed her on the cheek. Fiona smiled and gave a satisfied 'mmmmmm'.

"Good morning, Mr Robbins!" She sleepily raised her head, kissed me, and then clamped her legs around my left thigh.

"Hello, my darling!" I gently used the tip of my finger to trace an imaginary line from her chin, down her neck, "I could stay here all day!"

"Mmm, so could I! But what could we do?" That cheeky glint was back. She then obviously noticed that breakfast was in the adjoining room. "Do I smell bacon?" All of a sudden my thigh was no longer top of her agenda and she leapt out of bed, threw on a bathrobe and scuttled off to find some food.

I put my hands behind my head, leant back and gave a contented sigh. Neef returned with what was obviously a sharing platter of assorted breakfast items. She pulled off her robe and got back into bed. I could do this every day!

Later that morning we checked out of the hotel, drove over to Ticehurst to pick up Seamus and to say a quick 'hi' and 'bye' to the kids before we set off on our trip. With Seamus in tow we headed of back to my seaside house at Winchelsea Beach. We got home to find hotel and pub guides, thoughtfully given to us as presents by the family. We could spend the rest of our Sunday working out where we wanted to visit. The initial agreement was to go clockwise around the country, on the proviso that we had free rein to go in a different direction if we so wanted.

The rest of the day was spent with me resting, as I wanted to keep my strength up for the trip. I realised that I missed sharing my bed with someone. It's something that made, as I put it, an old man very happy indeed.

On Monday morning we set off in the van, with the plan of heading to the New Forest. However, as we reached the northern end of Southampton we both agreed that 'North' was the answer and turned off onto the M3 to Winchester, not to view the fabled Round Table that hung in the City Hall, nor to view the statue of Alfred the Great who, rumour had it, burnt his buns when he got too close to the fire once, but from there on to Newbury, then Oxford and finally arriving in Stratford-upon-Avon. We parked up and checked in to a lovely riverside hotel, sauntered around the town and dined in a lovely restaurant.

Tuesday saw us in the city of Lincoln. My, what a flat county it seemed, with one exception, the majestic cathedral set up on top of the hill above the city. We found a little lane that called itself 'Steep Hill' and laughed it off as some local in-joke. When we got to the top, ten minutes later, we were delighted to find a wonderful Tudor-style pub in which we could rest our weary bones. Steep was an understatement!

That part of the country proved a fantastic area to explore. The Peak District, the Pennines, Yorkshire – we ended up in Bradford one day because we suddenly wanted to dine in a curry house. That night we relaxed in a beautifully relaxing country hotel, not a stone's throw from Leeds/Bradford airport – I never knew such places existed!

A longer journey came next, right up through the country to the wilds of Glasgow. Not, as Fiona initially thought, because I wanted to spend a wild night among the different shades of bacchanalia on Sauchiehall Street, but because I knew there were some fantastic restaurants up that way, restaurants that I wanted to visit one last time. It saddened me a little that this was turning into a kind of valedictory tour. What would happen at the end? Would that be time for me to ready myself to meet my maker? My affairs were in order, and I had changed my will in favour of Fiona, whilst still making provisions for Ellen, Lizzy and Peter, but what would I do when I got home? I get bored easily at the best of times, and I wasn't ready to sit around waiting for myself to die.

The journey down from Scotland took in the Lake District, North Wales, which included a wonderfully little train journey up a mountain from a sunny Porthmadog to a rain-soaked Blaenau Ffestiniog, and also a trip to Portmeirion, where I was able to proclaim, 'I am not a number, I am a free man, and so's my wife!' Hereford proved to be a delightfully sleepy little city, with its cathedral and the historic Mappa Mundi, a medieval depiction of the world on a huge sheet of vellum, as well as a Tudor-style house in the middle of the 'High Town' pedestrian area, and then the trip extended into a third week, with a trip to Ireland, to give me the chance to see Fiona's homeland, and then it was eventually time to come home, finally visiting the New Forest, of course.

On our way home we sat in the van up at Beachy Head, ate fish and chips for lunch and discussed what we should do with the rest of our time. Of course Fiona wanted to complete more pencil sketches – she only had a dozen or so at the moment- but how should we spend our time? I was officially retired from my job, due to ill-health, which was a deliciously understated euphemism, and so I resolved to use my accountancy skills to take care of Fiona's books, as she professed to not having the slightest idea as to what she could claim, what she could off-set, or what she could put down to an 'act of God'.

Back to earth with a bump

The morning after our return home, I was slightly less than delighted to receive a missive from the hospital, who deemed this an appropriate moment to send me two pieces of communication. The first, slightly more important one, was informing me of an appointment for a scan and general check-up, I dare say hopefully to check that Malcolm was still as shriveled as he was last time. The second missive raised my ire more than just a little bit. It was a 'customer service' questionnaire. I mean, a questionnaire, for God's sake. Instead of binning it, I opened it up and read Question One:

"How would you describe your visit to our hospital?"

I paused, then took a pen out and wrote 'Bloody painful, what do you think?" I then put the form in the prepaid envelope, and slipped it into my centre tray, the one marked 'LBW'. Yes, I have three trays, one marked 'In' and one marked 'Out'. The middle tray is reserved for those companies and individuals who right royally piss me off. 'LBW' stands for 'Let the Bastards Wait'.

The next task was to do as Neef not such much wanted, as needed. Her paperwork was shocking, so I did some collating and refilling, getting figures together and creating a spreadsheet. When it comes to bookkeeping I certainly do, as she put it, 'know my shit!' I could pore over figures for ages, devising formulae and making everything ship-shape. While I was busy organising Fiona crept up behind me and suddenly swivelled my office chair around. Then she plonked herself in my lap and said 'what you doin'?' I was tempted to say I was splitting the atom, but simply explained that I was trying to make some sense of her accounts and that, as far as I could make out at this early stage, she was owed some money.

I smiled, and then winced in pain, and had to take a couple of deep breaths. Fiona was concerned and came and gave me a hug, the kind of cuddle that meant 'let me take some of your pain away from you'. This trip to the hospital couldn't come too soon!

And so the day came when we trundled off with trepidation to see what the latest was with regards to my cancer. Now she was my wife, there would be no problem with Fiona coming into the consulting room with me. She waited impatiently as I was put through the spin cycle in the scanner, and then we waited together for the outcome. Mr Sadiq came over to us and ushered us into his office. He sat and pushed his glasses to his forehead.

"Mr Robbins, I would firstly like to congratulate you on your marriage to Mrs Robbins. Mrs Robbins, may I offer you my congratulations and warmest wishes, too." Fiona and I held hands and smiled at one another. We both had a feeling that this was not going to be a festival of positive news. "As regards your illness there appears to have been some growth in the size of the tumour on your pancreas. Disappointingly there also seem to be secondary metastases on your lungs."

"So what do we do now? More chemotherapy?"

"It is with great regret that I fear not, Mr Robbins. You are going to experience varying degrees of pain in the future, from a dull ache to a piercing, stabbing feeling. It will lay you very low indeed and, I am afraid that another course of chemotherapy will make you very weak indeed, and strangely may even act to shorten your life. I can, though, prescribe gemcitabine to help with symptoms, but it is not guaranteed that your body will be able to stand it."

Fiona and I looked at one another and we hugged and kissed. "My advice to you both, Mr and Mrs Robbins, is to make sure that all your affairs are in order and to make the most of the days you have together. I am so sorry I cannot offer you better news. I think we are looking at another 3-6 months at the most."

This may have sounded a bit bleak and abrupt, but I was grateful for Mr Sadiq's openness. Fiona and I now knew exactly what we were up against. Twelve to thirteen weeks as a minimum, but hardly likely to be more than 26 weeks. There's nothing like a deadline – bugger me, what a word – to clarify the mind.

"Let's go and eat! I said to Fiona as we left the hospital.

"Okay, are we going to talk about this?"

"Of course. Neef, my love, we can either sit and wait or carry on and fight the fight." It seemed strange that I was the feisty one now. I realised then that my darling Fiona was hurting. I pulled over into a convenient lay-by, switched off the ignition and took her in my arms, giving her an enormous kiss.

"Oh my darling, I am so, so sorry. I never ever want to leave you, and promise I will fight until there is nothing left to give."

Tears were streaming down from Fiona's eyes.

"Eeyore, I never, ever want to think about losing you."

"I don't want you to lose me. I cannot bear not being with you. So, if we are not going to eat, what shall we do?

There was a glint returning to her eyes. "Let's go home, go to bed, and eat."

How could I resist?

God Only Knows

As I lay there in bed with my wife in my arms, I couldn't help but notice that life is good when we are together. There's nothing in the world I need worry about, as Neef lies with her head on my chest. I listen to her contented breathing; see that contented smile on her face as she seems to nod on my chest, even if her eyes are closed. I never, ever thought that I could be this happy. My cancer can go and get stuffed, for all I care.

Fiona woke up from her nap, kissed me on the chest and looked up at me, to find me looking adoringly back at her.

"Hello, sleepyhead!"

"Eeyore, tell me now, how long have I been asleep for, and how long have you been watching me sleep?"

"For an instant, and an eternity, my darling."

"You smooth talker, you!" Fiona got out of the bed and walked to the bathroom. She returned and put the radio on. There wasn't any particular reason for doing this, but she thought, quite rightly, that some background music might be in order. "Want to listen to anything in particular?"

"The choice is yours, my love." She put the radio on to one of those stations that plays a selection of music from a variety of eras.

The first song on the radio was 'I Don't Like Mondays', we giggled together and I took her in my arms as she returned to the bed. The song played on a little.

"Did your daddy always say you were good as gold?" I asked her with a saucy hint to my voice.

"Oh, kind sir, I am always a good girl, unless I am in the company of a very bad man!" That earned a very passionate kiss.

Well, one thing led to another, as it does if you are a lucky person indeed, and then we lay there, a little while later, breathless and sweaty in one another's arms. We smiled at one another. I kissed Neef's nose, which wrinkled instinctively. I adore her so much!

Fiona looked at me, and then leant up on her elbows, looking down at me with an increasing look of worry. The music that had started in the background was The Beach Boys' 'God Only Knows'. At first she was calm, and then as the lyrics went on, she collapsed onto the bed, sobbing.

There were tears in my eyes too. Fiona was crying and there appeared to be no way to console her. I slipped an arm under her and she leaned back so that both my arms were around her. I held her so tight, and did the only thing I knew how, and that was rest my chin on her left shoulder, trying with my whispers to make my wife feel strong.

"Hey, shhh, I know, I know. It's a crappy song when you are in a situation like this. Sheer musical gold, but sheer emotional shite. Hey, come here, it's ok, I am not going anywhere in *a long while."*

"D'you mean that? Really? 'Cause I don't know what I'll do when you go. The longer you are here, the harder it will be, but also the stronger I will be. Does that make sense?" Fiona's sobbing had subsided now, but she lay there, shivering and shuddering as we all do after a bout of prolonged and profound crying.

"When the time does eventually come, we'll find a way of giving you the lasting memories you want, but there won't be any need for this for a long, long time. I wonder what song is coming next. Here we go." It was the Bellamy Brothers

That's more like it, I thought, as I let Fiona roll on to her back and I raised myself over her.

Getting my shit together – September 2011

It was then that I decided that I needed to get my shit together. I had scribbled down random jottings as I had progressed, or should that be regressed, through my illness. My aim wasn't some altruistic search to create a 'self-help guide' for cancer sufferers. I would never say that I have been brave about this. It's always the way that sufferers are portrayed at the end, after they have gone, probably because they are not in a position to argue about it. But no, courage has not been how I have felt. I've been scared, literally scared shitless at times. I have cried, I've wept buckets, both on my own, with my children, and of course with Fiona and with Seamus, sometimes all together, too. These journal writings have become a means of expressing to those closest to me what is actually going on my head as I journey on towards my end, and how much I love them all.

Yes, the abiding feeling I have had is love. Even though I have had some very dark days, some days when I have not been the most gracious or polite person in the English-speaking world, but I have felt loved. The love of my mum, even if she does still think she has to come and fuss around me, even if it has lessened now that I am a married man again, and that of my sister and brother and all the other assorted members of the Robbins clan scattered around the place. The love of my children is something which has been an absolute blessing. They are growing up so quickly – but I suppose that circumstances like those that we are all facing do force them to grow up quickly. I don't want them to lose their child-like innocence, though. Then again, I have just realised how stupid that sounds, as they are children. The one who has surprised me is Peter. He's stoic and yet seems to be rising to the challenge of growing into the role of 'man of the family'. Ellen is just calm and reassuring, showering love on Fiona and myself whenever she gets the chance. Lizzy knows that this story is not going to have a happy ending, but she continues to treat it as an abstract and absurd concept. Every time she sees me she lifts my shirt, stares at my abdomen and growls at it, saying 'bugger off, Malcolm!' You've got to love her!

Don't worry, I haven't forgotten the other one. Neef and I grow stronger together as each day passes. I am so determined not to leave her that we seem to spend every waking hour in each other's company. I took her for a ride on a steam train, mainly because it evoked childhood memories for me and also because it seemed like a good idea for a day out. We drove to Tenterden, which is another lovely little town in the Kentish Weald, not far from my home-town of Cranbrook. The smell of smoke and steam as we parked up at the station was unmistakeable and I was raring to go. We climbed aboard and sat, hand in hand, with an air of expectation, waiting for the off. Eventually the train started to move, and I could see the puffs of engine smoke passing by the window as the sun streamed through our carriage window. The train passed through the beautiful Wealden countryside, through Rolvenden, where the railways seemed to store its locomotives. Then we stopped briefly at Northiam, and then we passed the beautiful Bodiam Castle and the engine turned round. It was wonderful. I felt as if I had no cares in the world, even my terminal illness seemed to be a distant memory.

On the way back I decided we should get off for a while at Northiam, mainly because I had a memory I wanted to check up on. I seemed to recall that, not far from the station, there was a pleasant pub where we could locate some decent food and, far more importantly, a decent drop of ale. And so it proved to be – about five minutes' walk away we found it. We sat in the beer garden and I seemed to relax for the first time in what seemed like aeons. Fiona looked stunning that day – floaty skirt, flowery top, sunglasses and she was also wearing the things that had first struck me about her on that day we met at Beachy Head, her purple Doc Martens. She seemed to be blooming. Her (to me) extremely attractive curves were highlighted by the sunlight. She was drawing yet another sketch of me. That seemed to happen as a matter of course nowadays, as I was no longer so self-conscious about them. Neef looked up from her sketch book, looked at me, and smiled, a broad beaming smile that made me fall in love with her all the more. She seemed totally free of stress, which for me was like a weight lifted off of my shoulders.

A light lunch, and a pint of Harveys Sussex Best (of course) followed, then it was time to stroll down to Northiam Station to catch the train to Tenterden Town, once again stopping at Rolvenden before we made our way up the hill into Tenterden Town station.

This was a day that was vital. Since we got back from our honeymoon it had all been hospital, doom, gloom, worry and anxiety, interspersed with frequent sessions of 'rest' for the two of us. However, there had always been that ominous spectre looming, about which we could, if we wanted, talk freely to one another. Indeed I felt more free talking to Fiona than anyone else, not even Al and I had been as open as this during our marriage. The trouble was we didn't want my illness to be the central topic of conversation. We were adamant that we would make the best of everything and, if possible, try to carry on as if the Grim Reaper wasn't lurking around the corner, but it was very difficult at times.

Today, however, was an exception. We joked that, with the sunny weather, old Death himself had cleared off to Marbella on holiday, and we asked him not to send us a postcard. The thing was, while he was away, would it be possible to make a permanent break for freedom?

Well, it may have seemed utterly stupid and the most absurd thing ever, but we decided to give it a go. As we drove home to Winchelsea Beach, we wondered how on earth we could ever manage it, but we were sure we would give it a bloody good try.

Lumps and Bumps

Well, that's not exactly the most inspiring chapter title, is it? It does mean, though, that things have been (yet) more uneventful. I would waffle on, but I will spare you a diatribe on my illness yet again.

We had a shock last week. Fiona rushed into my study and threw herself into my arms, sobbing and shaking.

"It's Seamus!"

"What's up with him? Is he okay?

"I don't know. There's this thing on him, under his fur."

"What?"

"You know, one of them! A lump! I don't know what the feck I would do if I lost both of you one after another!"

"Let me take a look at him," I got up put of my seat, and strolled through to the living room where Seamus was lying, in his usual place, in front of the fire. Strange that, he would often lay in front of the fire even if it was the height of Summer and it wasn't *actually* lit, "Now then, Seamus, let's have a look at you then, shall we? Where's this lump then, love?"

Fiona indicated that it was on his flank, on the left hand side, about halfway between his front and hind leg. I ran the smooth of my palm along in search of it. It took a moment but then... Bingo! It was about the size of a fifty-pence piece, roundish, and definitely there. Seamus seemed completely oblivious to it all. He was happy to receive the attention. Like the old tart he was, he gave a moan and rolled on to his back, in the hope of getting his tummy tickled.

"Right. Well, you're correct, there is a lump there, but it obviously isn't hurting him. If you hadn't terminated his night-club membership when he was a pup I dare say he'd be leaping up and trying to rodger me! I am not sure what it is, but let's get it checked out by the vet".

So we all got in the car that afternoon and took Seamus off to see Miss McAndrew, my local vet. I hadn't seen her in a while, not since my own dog had had to be put down, in fact. We explained what we had found on Seamus' body, and she gave him an examination. Fiona and I held each other for what seemed like ages. The silence was deafening. Finally, it was broken by Miss McAndrew, and we were delighted to hear her diagnosis of an accumulation of fatty tissue, which was benign and nothing to worry about. She gave us the option of removing the lump, but Fiona and I decided that having one member of the family under the knife was more than enough and, if it wasn't going to hurt or bother Seamus in the least, there would be no sense in him undergoing an operation needlessly. We breathed a huge sigh of relief, and both hugged Seamus.

It was so good to go to bed that night knowing that the dog was going to be okay. Fiona and I lay there, and gazed into one another's eyes. There was no need to speak. We could see from each other's look that there was collective relief. I kissed Neef on the forehead and she nuzzled down into my chest to fell asleep.

Excuse me for being graphic, but I've always been notice that people throw up in different ways. My dad was silent about it, and the only time I ever saw him throw up was after a heavy night at a works' party, he staggered into the house in silence, then wobbled upstairs and toppled into the bathroom. After a couple of minutes of rhythmic retching, couple with moans of 'leave me, I want to die', he then fell asleep with his head rested against the no doubt cooling porcelain of the toilet. My brother, on the other hand, will make sure everyone hears about it. I am certain his spewing would be investigated by the Noise Abatement Society.

So what led me to this ever-so fragrant description of the vagaries of vomit? That next morning, I woke up to what I thought was the sound of gentle coughing. I walked to where the sound was coming from, and found Fiona being daintily 'ill'. I wasn't sure if this was indeed Neef's very own 'vomiting style' or whether she didn't want to disturb me and, anyway, this was not the time or place to ask. I rubbed her back and made sure none of her wild, red hair was dangling anywhere near the trajectory of her vomiting. I made sure that I did not ask her if she was alright, as she very clearly was not. I did, though, say the one thing that I had maintained I would never say.

"Come on, get it all out, you'll feel better."

"Do you know how fecking useless that phrase is?"

I am surprised Fiona didn't give me a swift elbow to the balls for that crass comment. She raised her head, wiped away the sweat from her brow and the extraneous flecks of vomit from her chin. She told me that she did feel better, but she didn't know what was wrong. I immediately worried that she was suffering from exhaustion and this was her body's reaction to the stresses and strains of living with a man who is terminally ill. We weren't absolutely sure what was wrong, and so resolved to fix Fiona up with an appointment at the doctor's as soon as we could. The one we scheduled was a couple of days off, and so we coped with a couple more days of vomiting. Well, I didn't have to cope, as I was not the one being ill, but I can empathise, can't I?

My local GP's surgery is, as I related at the beginning of my journal, not my idea of a pleasant day out. There were no female doctors available, so we had arranged to see Dr Matthews, with whom I still had a good relationship and who had, by now, become a very good friend to me and to Fiona. We explained the symptoms and the good Doctor looked pensive.

"Tell me, Fiona, are you on the Pill?"

"Well, sure I am, but that shouldn't be any worry, except to my old parish priest in County Wicklow, should it?"

"None at all. Have you had any stomach bugs in the last couple of months?"

"Well, I had a minor tummy bug about 6 weeks back. I had a chicken jalfrezi that didn't agree with me. Too many green chilli peppers, you know?"

"Do you use other forms of contraception to minimise the risk of transferring chemotherapy drugs?"

"Oh yes, we use condoms, which normally work, albeit with one or two failures."

"In which case I suggest," Dr Matthews' face looked serious. I was really worried now, "that I ask you to step into the toilet for a sec and do me the courtesy of peeing on this pregnancy testing kit."

Fiona and I looked at each other, dumbfounded. As she had been on the Pill we hadn't even contemplated pregnancy, especially as symptoms like a missed period would not be evident. She took the testing kit that the doctor handed her, and stepped off in a sprightly manner to do what she had to do. I was pensive, and had lots of questions, but decided that I would wait until any definitive diagnosis before I should raise them.

A couple of minutes later, Fiona returned and handed over the little plastic container that held the wand that would give us the answer. We had to wait a minute or so. Dr Matthews was the one who cracked.

"I can't stand this bloody suspense, can you?" He lifted up the kit, looked at the indicator screen, and raised an eyebrow. "Well, there's your answer," he said, turning the indicator to face us. There, in the little window, were two clearly visible vertical blue lines, "congratulations, you two! Seamus is going to have a little brother or sister!"

I am not good at being dumbfounded for long, and so I felt it appropriate to ask the questions that had decided to plague me since the prospect of pregnancy had first made an appearance a few minutes earlier. I asked whether my age would have any bearing on the health of the baby, and whether my illness could in anyway harm my unborn child. As you can see, I may be good at being an accountant, but the human body holds many a mystery to me. The doctor assured us that the prospect of both was minimal, but he would arrange some tests to make sure there had been no problems with the chemo drugs. He then got up and shook me by the hand, and then kissed Fiona on the cheek. See, I told you he was a family friend!

Fiona had remained silent throughout. Once we left the medical centre, we went home, and decided to we had to discuss the 'situation', as I so depressingly put it. Fiona wasn't angry, and was happy, in part at least. I think the problem was partly that she hadn't even considered pregnancy, in her marriage to me or even in her previous marriage. Her ex-husband 'wasn't a great husband, so he'd have been a fecking crap father', as she put it. The thing that worried Neef was actually, quite straightforward. How could she go through a pregnancy that I, in all probability, would not be around to see the end of? Would she have the emotional capacity to cope? If she could just about cope with losing me, how would an infant cope with her emotions as it would be a reminder of the man she had loved and lost, as it were? I certainly was in no position to counter any worries by insisting on any course of action.

"So, are you saying you'd like to consider a termination?"

"Would you like me to?"

"Oh bugger, no! The issue does remain, though, that we hadn't factored children into the equation."

"I know, Eeyore, I know, but there's one overarching thing as well. I may be a lapsed catholic girl, but I am still a catholic girl at heart. That and the fact that if I were to consider an abortion I'd feel like I were killing you again, and I can't even abide the thought of you going once, let alone twice. No, it's a shock, but we will cope, and I will cope, and Junior will be a positive memento of our life together, and not some tragic vestige."

She got up out of her armchair, and coolly walked over to mine. She removed her blouse and held her bare abdomen close to my face. "Sure, daddy Eeyore, would you like to say hello to the new addition to our little family?"

I tenderly kissed Neef's belly and held it close to my face. I will never forget the feel of her delicate, white, soft skin against my own. Even though it always looked cold, it exuded a warmth that I always felt exhilarating and exciting, and would so until my dying day.

Blown away

Fiona here. Feck me, it's been a while since I have written anything to go in this journal. Today, though, has been such a heartbreaking and simultaneously heartwarming day that I felt compelled to write something, at least.

Let's see now, I started the day throwing my fecking guts up and ended it learning that I was going to have a baby. How did that happen?

A baby, eh? Well, that was a shocker, that's for sure. Until today I can safely say that I have never had any maternal feelings whatsoever. I never was any good at relationships, and my marriage was such a fecking disaster that children would have just muddied the waters. If I think now, and Peter is fast asleep in our bed so I have the chance to, I must admit that I am delighted by the idea of a junior Robbins cooking away inside my belly. Who knows what it is going to be, boy or girl, twins or rugrat, but it is ours. I cannot actually think of any more fitting thing to remember Peter by. We are creating our own little life, we have created it even. We will see what the future holds, but when that dreaded day comes when my beloved Eeyore leaves me I know that there will be something, or should I say someone, to remember him by.

It's 2am and Seamus wonders what the feck I am up to, but I am stroking my tummy like there's no tomorrow, proving to Junior that his, or her, mammy and daddy love him to bits, and he or she will be loved in the future by me, and I will tell him about daddy, who is the loveliest daddy that anyone could ever ask to meet. It's getting chilly now, I'd best get back to my bed to warm my tummy on daddy to keep junior warm.

Do you know the way to scan José?

Bugger me, but doesn't the prospect of a new addition to the family add complications? First of all we had to find out when Junior was going to arrive on the scene, and this required a visit to meet our midwife, Sue Watkins. Sue was a diminutive woman. Now, when I say diminutive you probably think she is around five feet two inches. Well, for Sue you need to subtract another four inches. She's so small that, when she said she needed to examine Fiona's business end, I thought she was going to don a snorkel and wetsuit and climb up to carry out a first-hand inspection. I decided not to share this information in the clinic, as I deemed that it may be considered coarse and unacceptable. You may have noticed that I try not to be coarse. Anyway, Sue carried out her inspection and came up for air (sorry, couldn't resist). She informed us that, as far as she could tell, Neef was ten weeks gone, leaving us around thirty weeks to go. There's nothing like that to clarify the mind. I immediately did the calculation. I was now thirteen weeks past the initial cut-off point indicated to me by Mr Sadiq, and he said that I was likely to see another thirteen weeks before my illness finally got the better of me. Even though this should have been the brightest, most wonderful moment of my marriage to Fiona, we now had the prospect of me not being around for the birth of Junior, as I will probably have died ten weeks beforehand. All together now... bugger!

Fiona could see that I was a little worried, and instinctively knew what I was worrying about. She took me by the hand and said 'it's gonna be okay, Eeyore'. Sue also sensed the tension, and we explained the situation. She was sympathetic, offered to do home visits from now on, and then lightened the mood by asking if we wanted to hear Junior's heartbeat.

Wow! She set up the sound monitor and found exactly the right spot on Fiona's stomach. She had a listen for herself first of all, and she looked a little concerned. Neef and I looked at each other, utterly bemused. Was this moment of happiness about to be dashed from the very start?

Sue shrugged her shoulders and switched on the speaker attached to the ultrasound device. It was indistinct at first, but eventually we could make out a distinct heartbeat, beating around as if it was knocking frantically on a door.

"Now, I don't want to worry you, but it appears that there is a lot of noise down there." Sue said quietly. "Do your families have any instances of twins?"

Neef and I looked at one another and burst into broad and beaming smiles. A scan was booked for the next day at the Conquest Hospital in Hastings. The Conquest is a fairly modern hospital, set up on the hill above the town. We went into the Obstetrics department and waited for our turn. Eventually we went in and they wired Fiona up. They checked her blood pressure and then set about the task at hand. The listened to the sound of the heart, or indeed hearts, beating inside Neef's abdomen. The next step was to take a photo of what was going on down there. This required a careful manoeuvring of the sensor, but at last they had a decent image. The nurse showed us exactly what was going on. She pointed out hands, legs, arms, and eventually two different heads down there, curled up together inside Fiona's womb.

My heart soared. Sure, two babies for a relatively recent widow would be more problematic, but the plus points were that there's be twice the memories of me, twice the warmth, and twice the demonstration of the love that Fiona and I felt for one another. Of course I was thinking this to myself, as I would have to discuss this with Neef once we got home. As we were around ten weeks of pregnancy, we didn't know what gender the babies were, that would have to wait a few weeks, it seemed.

Once we got home, Fiona and I sat down to discuss what I referred to as 'double top'. I explained that I was ostensibly happy, but of course I would not be around to deal with one newborn baby, let alone twins. Fiona cried at first, as this was yet another emotional shock for her, even if it wasn't going to be a physical one for a little while. However she was happy, which was an understatement. We were comfortably off, and she knew that she would be happy to have two physical, if noisy, and frequently hungry and beshitted, small people by which to remember me.

That night, I held Neef in my arms, resting my left hand on where I imagined her bump would be, and as she was having a brace of Juniors I guessed it wouldn't be long before there was a bump. We decided to shoot the breeze as we lay there, trying to work out how we would refer to our unborn arrivals. I had already been comfortable with Junior, but now there were two of the little blighters, it would require a little thought.

"How about Tweedledum and Tweedledee?" Fiona suggested. It was along the right lines but a little long in terms of the syllables, I suggested. She said I was too fecking fussy, a comment that was accompanied by a kiss to my chest.

"Tom and Jerry? Pinky and Perky? Homer and Ned?" She rattled these off very quickly indeed.

"How about Dave and Nick?" I suggested, thinking of an unlikely partnership in Westminster.

"You can piss right off with that one!"

"Let's be thankful it's not Hughie, Dewey and Lewey!"

"You're right there," she said, "sure I love you with all my heart, but I am not sure how I'd cope with three."

"Let's find a definitive answer then, one we can both agree on"

We thought for a second, and then both suggested, almost simultaneously...

"Laurel and Hardy!"

The best-laid plans

Well, it would not be a surprise to say that the next few weeks were not uneventful. Each morning was begun by me comforting Fiona as she threw up into the toilet for an hour or so. Then we tended to have a light breakfast, and out of consideration for my wife's delicate state in the mornings I tended to forsake my occasional need for the 'full English' – eggs, bacon, sausage, fried bread, tomato and black pudding – as the sight of Neef turning green was not the most comforting of sights for me, such was my love for her.

We took things easy. I would read or write, and Fiona would sketch me. I was still feeling fairly chipper, although I had noticed that I was losing a lot of weight. I weighed myself one day and, for a man of six feet three inches, I was shocked to see I was now eight and a half stone. Well I be buggered – I was feeling okay, but I was starting to waste away like there was no tomorrow. It was certainly a marker that the countdown had started and, strangely, it was something that I chose not to share with Fiona. She had enough to cope with, with Laurel and Hardy cooking away inside her belly – I didn't want to add to her worries.

Eventually the time came for the next scan. We had decided to find out what flavour the babies were, mainly so we could get things prepared for their arrival. Yes, I know that my family said that we shouldn't jump the gun and organise things too soon, but I was dying, for God's sake. How much bad bastard luck can one family have? Anyway, back to the hospital we went. Fiona wanted for Laurel and Hardy to be two little boys, which was something that sent me into an impromptu celebration of one of Rolf Harris' hits, whereas I was easy-going, perhaps with a slight preference to having two more daughters, even if that would leave Peter seriously outnumbered. Well, we went in for the scan and they got the exciting machines out.

As we were both Monty Python buffs, we asked if they had got the most expensive machine in the hospital in there, along with the machine that goes 'ping', but the staff in the obstetrics department looked utterly bemused. They scanned Fiona and, lo and behold, our thoughts were totally scuppered yet again. It turned out that we were not expecting two boys, or two girls, but one of each.

It's never straightforward is it? No sooner had we decided on Laurel and Hardy as two names, then the little blighters go and prove that to be wrong. So we needed to come up with a suitable set of names, which was not an onerous task, as we were still overjoyed by the prospect of two small people being born to us. I wondered what we should term them – Brucie and Tess, Paul and Debbie, George and Gracie or Posh and Becks. Who cares, what is important is that my darling Neef is fine and well and, above all, happy with what lies ahead for the both of us.

Hitting the rocks

And so it came to pass. Here I was with a stunning wife with whom I was delighted to be spending my last days. She was happily incubating Posh and Becks in her abdomen (yes, we had opted for the post-ironic celebrity names) and, along with Seamus, we were having the time of our lives. How can I term it? We pottered along. No big song and dance numbers, no long road trips, but just enjoying our days, enjoying life, enjoying each other, both socially, spiritually and, yes, still physically. Fiona's bump was getting progressively larger, so we had to find ways to enjoy one another that required a little more acrobatic movement on both our parts.

Neef is starting to feel uncomfortable with the two bairns under her skin. She isn't tiny, but she isn't large, and therefore having two unborn children growing up inside of her is bound to become a little cramped, isn't it?

I have completely lost track of where we are in terms of my illness, which in some ways is a blessed release. I have no idea whether I am ahead of schedule or not. When I say ahead of schedule I mean looking like I am going to pop my clogs sooner than planned. When I say 'no idea' that's not exactly true. When Fiona was diagnosed as being in 'le club pudding' I had reached my three-month cut-off. That was November 5th. It's now January 6th, nine weeks later, which means Fiona is now nearly five months' pregnant, and I have about a month left to live.

I will let you into a little secret, though. I am determined to try and be around for the birth of my children. That is not to say that the pain in my abdomen is not there. Pain is pretty constant, although it does subside when Neef comes up with a physical activity to take my mind off it. Nudge nudge, wink wink, say no more, as Eric Idle would suggest! I need to get three months past what I have laughingly called 'D-Day' to do it. They say a lot about a positive mental attitude, and I refuse to give in, especially as there is such a tangible prize at the end of it.

There have been some lighter moments, of which one immediately springs to mind. Just before Christmas I was having a lie down on the sofa, awaiting a maternal visitation, and not in a little pain. Sue, the midwife came to do her regular check-up on Neef and the twins, and decided to compliment me, with a cheeky nudge to my leg, on my ability to take things easy. Cheeky mare! Anyway, as she left, my dear old mum was walking down the street. The doorbell rang and Fiona opened the door to welcome her mother-in law into the house for her visit. All my mum could say was 'I see the midwife was late this morning!' to which I, in the middle of a small bout of intense pain, bellowed out 'We'll get her to effing well clock in next time, if that helps!' Either mum didn't hear me or she chose not to answer, so the visit didn't start out as a total disaster.

A couple of days later I awoke in the early hours of the morning to find my beloved Fiona doubled-up in pain in the bed. She was weeping uncontrollably, and it took a while to get any sense out of her.

"Neef, darling, what's wrong?" I asked.

"Oh, Eeyore!" she sobbed, and I could just about make out what she was saying, "My stomach hurts so much, and I am bleeding! I am so scared I am losing the babies!"

"Why didn't you wake me?!" I wasn't angry with her, how could I be? I held her for a moment, telling her that we were going to get through it all and we'd all be fine. I grabbed my phone and called the Obstetrics department. They asked me if I could get Fiona to the Accident and Emergency department at the Conquest Hospital as soon as possible. They would send an ambulance if needed, but I thought that, with the distance from the ambulance station, plus my desire to protect Neef, along with Posh and Becks, meant that I would be happier to drive them all along the road to the hospital.

We were at the hospital within twenty minutes. I only hope that the speed cameras on the A259 weren't working. Well, if they were, sod them! I helped Neef into the A&E department- she was not in a condition to walk anywhere near briskly – and they were all set. They had been forewarned by the Obstetrics Department and had a cubicle ready with the necessary monitors and all the rest of the machines and drugs that they might need to call upon to make Fiona as comfortable as possible. The first thing they did, thankfully, was to reassure her to help her be calm, as calmness was going to be vital if we were going to keep Posh and Becks in our lives. I decided to keep any private fears I had to myself, as there's be plenty of time for worry etc with Fiona at another time.

The first piece of good news was that Neef had not suffered a miscarriage, but that wasn't to say that all was well. She was now twenty-two weeks pregnant – alarmingly soon if the medics were forced to deliver the babies prematurely, so the important tasks at the moment were to make sure that the babies were not in distress and that Fiona's body calmed itself down. Once she had been monitored for a couple of hours they decided to take her up to the Obstetrics Department ward – I wondered at first why they wouldn't take her to Maternity, but then I reasoned that they might want to keep worried, expectant mothers and fathers who are undergoing stressful times away from all the newborns who might increase stress levels and increase worry or, if the worst came to the worst, grief.

By this stage in the proceedings I was absolutely shattered. I sat in an armchair next to Neef's bed and pulled a blanket over me. I couldn't sleep at all, so much was my worry and concern for my wife, so I decided to just sit there, looking at her, showing her that look that I had when I used to watch her sleeping – the look that simply said 'I love you'. Night went, and as the early streaks of that wintry morning sunlight came stuttering through the curtains in Neef's room in the hospital, I could see she was asleep. The monitor attached to her abdomen showed, thankfully, two steadily rapid heartbeats. At the moment, it appeared, my babies would be okay. A nurse came in and did the necessary observations. She smiled weakly at me and then left. It was neither the time nor the place to indulge in 'small talk' and I was sure as hell not in the condition to dive into my usual brand of lunacy. At a little before ten o'clock Fiona's eyes opened and she looked like she wanted to talk to me.

"Hey, Eeyore," she croaked to me, "I feel like shit this morning. How are Posh and Becks?"

"Well, the doctor hasn't been round yet but there are still two hearts beating on the monitor."

"That's good... that's good. Oh shit, darling, I am so sorry,"

"What are you sorry about, there's no need. We're here and we are doing our damnedest to encourage the babies to stay where they are at the moment. Just try to relax and we will follow every instruction that the doctors give us."

"I love you, Eeyore"

"Neef, my darling, I love you too. Now rest."

Eventually a very nice registrar came to see us. She looked at Fiona's chart and thought deeply. It was the kind of thinking that immediately drew your attention to the sound of wheels slowly grinding into action. She thought for a little while longer until, just before I shouted 'for Christ's sake, say something!' she spluttered into vocal communication. She informed us that the twins were both okay but that it was unlikely that Fiona would get to full-term, as they were both 'above average' in size and they'd end up fighting for space in the womb, as the planning department hadn't opened yet for them to build an extension. So, the initial target was to get Fiona to 30 weeks, which would give Posh and Becks a far better chance to thrive when they did make their first appearance in the world. This also meant, of course, that my next intermediate target was to survive the next eight weeks, which surely should be feasible. If Fiona got to thirty-four weeks they would whip her in for a caesarean section and I would be a daddy again! Well, there was the second target – if I could manage eight, the least I could do was manage another four to be able to see my fourth and fifth child in the flesh. To get to thirty weeks would involve a weekly check up with the redoubtable Sue, who would keep us all in check. The prescription in the meantime was no mountaineering, no bungee jumping, just taking things gently. No undue excitement, I thought, which led me to ask the registrar if that meant that sex with me was still a possibility then – Neef gave me a whack on the arm for that one!

Slowly Slowly Catchy Baby

After a few days of rest and observation, Fiona was discharged from the hospital. We drove home to Winchelsea Beach and spent the rest of the day resting. I sauntered into the kitchen and knocked up something to eat with a drop of mineral water. Well, Neef had the water as she didn't mind me having a drop of beer.

Oh shit! I haven't told you about the biggest achievement of the last few months, have I? I had originally decided that, as I was going to die, there wasn't much point in giving up smoking, but when we learned that we were with child, and then eventually with children, I decided that, for the sake of the babies, I'd best at least try, as it would slightly increase the odds of me meeting my children when they eventually decided to make an entrance, as well as cutting out the smoke around Fiona with the associated risks of damage to the unborn as well as reducing the nausea that she had begun to suffer whenever I was puffing away around her. I have been a smoker since, well I hope you won't tell anyone, but since I was at primary school. I remember that day like it was yesterday – I was in class 1 at Cranbrook Junior school and I got caught having a crafty fag at the age of seven by Mr Griffiths, the caretaker. I received an immediate bollocking from him, was threatened with the cane by the headmistress, Miss Adamson, and then received a treble bollocking with an extra serving of the wooden spoon around my arse from mum and dad when they got home from work.

Bloody hell, that wooden spoon got a good workout from time to time. There's nothing like being a mischievous little sod to earn a swift whack. It never did me any harm, but those days are gone and, in my view at least, that's a good thing. There were times with my three that I was an exceptionally grumpy dad, but my bark was always worse than my bite. I could certainly be very grumpy at times, but I always eventually tried to explain to my children what it was about a certain deed or comment that had irked me. Personally speaking I always found that trying to reason with children worked – they'd try to understand, even if they often made the same mistake on more than one occasion. I have just realised that this seems like some pathetic attempt to write a child-rearing manual. All I can say is that it is not. Maybe my darlings – Ellen, Lizzy and Peter will understand a little of why their old dad did things the way he did after he had gone, but it's up to them to decide how they are going to react in their own ways if or when they become parents. As for Fiona, I would never presume as to how she should bring up Posh and Becks. She is such a wonderfully warm, generous and loving person that she won't need guidance, and besides she won't be wanting parenting tips from beyond the grave.

I dare say you will be reading this when I am gone, my darling. I know there will be days when the twins seem to go against every instinct you have and will drive you bonkers, but your love and instincts won't go far wrong. Of course I am sorry that I am not there to offer the wisdom of a wizened old fart, and I wish to God that I could be with you, but then again if I hadn't been diagnosed with a tumour I wouldn't have woken up to Seamus slobbering all over me all those months ago up at Beachy Head, would I?

I guess that I was coming to terms with all the different aspects of my life, good and bad, and in my own way I was making my peace with the world. I must admit that I am now feeling strangely at ease with everything. All those things that would have caused me to swear over the years I now look at and smile at, or, at worst, shrug my shoulders. I will never forgive myself, though, for the fact that I will be leaving Neef with two babies to look after. That, said, though, I know she will do the job wonderfully.

Anyway, back to reality, and six weeks later we decided that I had best go and see some members of the family that I hadn't seen in a while. I saw the kids and my mum and siblings on a fairly regular basis, but I hadn't been to Burgess Hill to see Auntie Maud in many a long year. She was now in her early nineties now and, thankfully, still in control of her faculties. We drove over to Burgess Hill, which is a pleasant dormitory town about 12 miles to the north of Brighton, and to the little complex of warden-assisted flats where Auntie Maud lives.

I pressed the buzzer that would, hopefully, allow us entry and, as I expected, it took a little while for Auntie Maud to come to the intercom. We entered the building and made our way to the lift to the third floor, where we would find Auntie Maud's flat. As we got there, the door opened and my auntie, a little lady with white hair and a pair of horn-rimmed spectacles came out to greet Fiona and myself. If I wanted a nice, warm, affectionate greeting I was to be sadly disappointed.

"Bugger me, you look rough! Hello Fiona, love. Is my nephew behaving himself?" As ever, Auntie Maud demonstrated the plain-speaking traits of our family. She ushered us inside and sat us down in her lounge while she toddled into the kitchen to make a pot of tea. Maud Robbins, the oldest-surviving member of the family, had never married, and was my dad's eldest sister, being eight years older than he was. It's not often you find a sprightly ninety-one year-old, let alone one who will offer banter and even mildly cheeky conversation with the young apprentices who worked in her local butcher's shop. It had been rumoured that Maud could make an infinite number of puns on the word 'fillet'. Her living room looked as if it hadn't changed in thirty years. The sofa and two accompanying armchairs had that old-fashioned tapestry-style fabric, and a display cabinet featured photographs of her siblings, nieces and nephews and numerous other relatives. She was the current custodian of the family bible, and probably knew where all the relevant skeletons were hidden, and in whose sheds the shovels were located. Neef and I looked at each other, both of us bemused by the olde-world-iness of it all and also by its inherent charm. Here was a little old lady who obviously thought a great deal of her family and who didn't care if she upset anyone with her attitude to life.

After a little while Auntie Maud waddled back into the living room carrying a tray that contained all the accoutrements of an elderly relative's 'entertaining kit' − a brown teapot with a multicoloured woollen tea cosy, cups and saucers, the kind that just about held a mouthful of scalding-hot liquid, and cake. Oh how I loved cake when it was baked well by my relatives. Sadly, over the years, Auntie Maud's baking efforts had the odd noticeable 'curiosity'. Today's effort was coffee sponge. The sponge itself was delightfully light and moist, and the coffee-flavoured butter icing was very pleasant in the main; however instead of using coffee essence or flavouring she had opted to use instant coffee granules, which led to me biting into a full-sized granule of raw instant coffee. Still, I smiled and told Auntie Maud that her cakes were as delightful and lovely as ever.

We chatted about many things, and in addition to our hopes for the future of Posh and Becks I also showed Auntie Maud some recent photographs of Ellen, Lizzy and Peter to show her how much they had grown. I am not so sure that Alex will take the children to see my elderly relatives, and I can't really rely on mum to do so as she is getting on now, so it is my fervent hope that Fiona will. Then again, I don't need to hope as I know that she will.

"You know what, Eeyore? I really love your family!" said Fiona delightedly as she drove us home. Yes, you read that right. I was feeling a little under the weather after the visit so I relinquished control of the Volvo to Neef. She was a decent driver, but the problem is that I am a slightly nervous passenger. I could be a passenger in a Sherman Tank and still feel nervous, so this wasn't a slight on my wife's abilities behind the wheel. We drove down onto the A27 and across the top of Brighton and down past the University of Sussex towards Lewes, Polegate and the coast road to Neef's flat, as we needed to sort out some bits and pieces in readiness for selling it, something we hadn't really cared about doing for a while, as it seemed so unimportant in the grand scheme of things. The winter sun was fading behind us but I still saw what I perceived to be a rosy glow about my wife, the kind of glow that had made me fall in love with her all those months ago, when Fiona removed her grey nightie to stand naked in front of me the night after I learned that my chemotherapy had been a success of sorts. That glow that I relished every single time we had delighted in each other's bodies. That glow that had become even deeper and more beautiful when we learned that Fiona was to become a mother, the mother of my twin babies.

I smiled contentedly, and didn't notice the headlights that were approaching us on the wrong side of the dual carriageway.

Aftermath

Apparently it was a teenage boy who was out trying to impress his friends. Apparently he had only just passed his driving test, and the most worrying thing for Neef and myself was that he had apparently had his brain and common sense removed when he passed it. There are only one or two things about which I am grateful in this life. Firstly I must apologise to Neef. She is actually a very good driver. As soon as she became aware of a care on a definite collision course with us, she took her foot off the accelerator and slowed the car a little, and then instinctively turned the steering wheel to the left. That meant that, instead of a head-on collision, the centre of the silver V-Reg Vauxhall Corsa connected fully with the front wing of the Volvo. I remember the sudden jolt, and the feeling that someone was smacking something into my back, accompanied by the detonation of the airbags in the car.

The second thing that I am so grateful for is that the car in which we were sitting was a Volvo. I am not so sure whether any other kind of car would have led to a more serious impact inside the cabin, but it did put up a very robust defence in order to protect its passengers.

At first, there was a deathly stillness, almost as if the whole world had shut down upon impact. All that was noticeable was the eerie mist from airbag gas. Once I realised that I was, to all intents and purposes, okay, my mind was immediately drawn to my driver, from whom there was no sound, I turned my head to her to see how she was. There didn't appear to be any physical injury, but her eyes were closed.

"Neef, are you there? Neef, are you okay? For Chris'sakes, Neef, say something!"

After what seemed like an eternity, but which in reality was about twenty seconds, Fiona's eyes flickered open and she looked towards me. She groaned.

"Bugger me, Eeyore, what happened there?"

"Some stupid bastard driving on the wrong side of the road. Don't move, I'll ring for an ambulance."

"Oh, do you think we need one?"

"What do you think?! How are Posh and Becks?"

"They're there, but they are right royally pissed off. Maybe an ambulance is sensible. Want me to get out of the car?"

"Don't move a bloody muscle. The paramedics will know how to move you. Now you're awake I am going to see what it looks like outside. Don't go anywhere!"

"That wasn't at the top of my agenda. I'm bursting for a piss, though."

I stepped gingerly out of the car. I was basically okay, just the odd niggle that meant that I would ache for a few days. The front wing of the Volvo had taken a pretty hefty impact. When the Corsa hit we were doing about twenty-five miles per hour. God knows how fast it was going, but the wing was totally crumpled back, but it had done its job, it seemed, in absorbing the energy of impact. I looked behind the car to see what had happened to the Corsa.

The crash had spun it round totally, so that it was now facing the correct, easterly direction. There was no sign of any life in the car, though. It appeared that there had been three occupants- the driver and a front and rear seat passenger. I'd never seen the real aftermath of an accident before, and it wasn't a pretty sight. If I hadn't been suffering from what was later diagnosed as mild shock, I'd have been so furious that I would have been trying to remonstrate with the driver for putting my wife's life, my unborn twins' lives, and my life in danger. I will still, though, surrounded by a fuzzy stillness, which made me feel like an observer and not an actual participant in this devastating scene.

As I neared the Corsa, I pretty much worked out that none of its occupants had been wearing seatbelts. The rear seat passenger had been catapulted forwards and out, through the windscreen. He lay there, his body half in, half out of the car, his face cut to ribbons by the broken windscreen glass, and not one breath in his body. The driver and front seat passenger had fared little better. The young driver – oh so young, I guess not much older than Ellen – was jammed up against the obliterated steering column. There wasn't much of that to see, as the steering wheel had deformed and a fair amount of all that had been thrust into his torso as the momentum of his rear passenger slammed his driver's seat forwards at I-don't-know-what speed. The young, female passenger was also clearly dead. Her seatback had been slammed forward, shoving her forwards towards the dashboard, with which I would guess her chin had made impact, jarring her head up and backwards so hard that I dare say her neck would have been instantly broken. All I could hope was that their deaths had been relatively instant.

"Children, just children", I said quietly to myself, and I immediately rushed back to see how Neef was. One of the drivers behind us had obviously made the necessary call to the emergency services as I could hear the wailing of sirens in the near-distance. I opened my door and told Fiona that the ambulance was on its way.

I was immediately scared by the fact that there was, once again, silence in the Volvo.

London on Sea

I bloody well hate Brighton. I know it has its charms, like the ostentation of the Royal Pavilion and the inherent charm and quaintness of The Lanes, but this is personal. Bad things always seem to happen to me there, from the time when I threw up as a ten year old at the Pool Valley Bus Station at Old Steine in front of a girl who I fancied, to today.

Today? Well, I was sitting in a room in the Obstetrics Department at the Royal Sussex County Hospital, watching my unconscious wife and worrying like nobody's business about her and our unborn twins. The twins were hanging in there, and we were lucky that the force of the collision had not brought labour forward.

When I had reached the car after the crash, to let Fiona know that the ambulance was on its way, she was not conscious. I tried to talk to her, but was so overwhelmed by upset that I started worrying. I am afraid to say that I swore at the paramedics, telling them to 'effing well get my wife out of my effing car'. Fortunately for me they were understanding and could see I was suffering from shock. Neef, it seemed, was suffering from severe concussion and she had fallen unconscious. I tried to reassure myself that her body was sleeping to help it repair itself. She had also broken her nose when her face connected with her airbag, but that was a minor matter.

The crash was yesterday evening, and it was now 6 a.m. For the last twelve hours I had been sitting there, either in the Accident and Emergency Department or in Obstetrics waiting, just waiting for my darling Fiona to come back to me. A nurse entered the room and checked the monitors. She swiftly walked outside and called for a doctor, who came in and checked what was going on.

He informed me that there appeared to be a degree of, as he termed it, 'foetal distress' and it was likely that they would have to go down to theatre to deliver the children.

My heart sank, as I was now consumed with an intense worry that none of them were going to survive.

The only thing that I could cling to in order to keep myself going was that the survival rate for births at twenty-eight weeks was ninety to ninety-five per cent, as opposed to seventeen per cent six weeks ago.

As I was recovering from shock, and was still suffering from terminal cancer, it was decided that I was not allowed in the operating theatre for the birth of my children. I sat in a day room and spent the next forty-five minutes staring intently at the floor, not noticing if anyone passed me or did anything in the room. The only break that I noticed was when a nurse stuck her head into the room to tell me 'your children have been born'. Was that it? No news on the condition of Fiona? No news on whether the twins were okay? I started pacing the room, and then picked up an empty coffee cup, threw it against the wall and kicked a gate-leg table in rage. Sadly I missed a bit and the edge of the table leaf smacked into my shin. I collapsed to the floor in agony, swearing at myself. I picked myself up off of the floor, wiped my eyes, and sat down and waited.

Eventually someone came to see me to explain what was going on. Thank Christ for that! The twins were okay. Well, when I say they were okay they were born three months premature and had been taken off to incubators in the Neo-Natal Care Unit. I was asked if I wanted to see them, but I said that I would rather wait and see my wife first. This, it seemed, was still not possible as Fiona was still undergoing surgery. My eyes widened in horror.

Apparently the delivery also highlighted injuries to Fiona's abdomen which were currently being explored and any action necessary was going to be taken. I was asked about consent, to which my answer was 'just keep Neef effing well alive to see me!' The doctor was confused, and then I realised that this wasn't my usual hospital. I explained my situation, the fact that I was terminally ill with only, in all probability a few more weeks to live, and how I loved my wife and my children and was consumed with worry. The doctor looked understanding and said that every single thing that was possible would be done to give Fiona the best chance possible. Apparently we'd know in about an hour how she was. I was asked once again if I wanted to see my children. I said I thought that would be a very good idea, and I also apologised about the damaged table leaf.

Bundles

I took the lift up to the Neo-Natal Care Unit. I was taken there by a nurse from the Obstetrics Department, who handed me over to the more than capable hands of a nurse from the Unit. She led me down the corridor, telling me how well the children looked and how she was confident that their premature birth would not pose any major problems in later life. We entered a small room and there they were, in two separate incubators, lay the two latest additions to my children. Bugger, I thought in a strangely whimsical manner, I'm now a father of five!

They looked so peaceful in their incubators. They slept as if they had not had any trauma in the last couple of days. They were so small, so perfect, so peaceful and, with their mother having god-knows-what surgery at this very moment in time, they were my very own little bundles of hope.

"Have you and your wife thought of names for your children yet?" The nurse asked. She knew what was going on but she wanted to help me concentrate on the here, the now, and not the inevitable what-ifs that the current situation brought with it.

"No, not at the moment," I murmured. I couldn't think much to speak – I was concentrating on my babies. They seemed to be a good size, and apparently both weighed in at about seven pounds even being born three months early. Posh, I'll still call them by their nicknames to make things easier at the moment, had a delightful snubbed nose and what looked like a cheeky smile, even when she was asleep. Her head was topped with a good quantity of what looked like auburn hair. 'Just like Neef', I thought to myself. Becks was a lean young man, with lean features and brown hair. They were just perfect. The nurse explained that they could provide for the children's every need while Neef was unwell, and suggested that, perhaps, now was a good time for me to go back to be with my wife. I agreed and returned to the Obstetrics Department.

When I returned to Obstetrics I was taken into a 'Families Room', where I was asked to wait until the surgeon came to see me. Now, there is one abiding thought that came to my mind. I am not one for the heaving bosoms of television drama, but from the one or two episodes of 'Casualty' that I have seen being placed in the Families Room means you have to be prepared for the worst. I sat, and pondered what possibilities might be ahead. I did not know if my wife of seven months was alive or dead, and I had two newborn children upstairs in incubators. Of course there was the minor inconvenience of the fact that I was due to die sometime before the summer kicked in. How would I cope with the twins without Neef? How would the twins cope knowing, eventually, that both their parents had died while they were infants? Who would care for the children?

The door to the Families Room opened and a familiar face looked in.

"Hey! How are you feeling?"

I must say that I was very surprised, but was also pleased to see this person. Members of my family would have been all over me and concerned and asking questions that I didn't particularly want to answer. With this person things would be different. We spoke about what had happened, from the crash, to Fiona's injuries to the birth of the children. I was listened to; I didn't have loads of probing questions thrown at me. I was listened to, I mean properly listened to, and I felt better. Well, I felt a little better at least.

That Letter

Royal Sussex County Hospital, February 15th 2012

Dear Alex,

I wanted to write to thank both you and James for popping in to see me at the hospital over here in Brighton. Believe me a pair of familiar faces were exactly what I needed to see. Thanks also for bringing over some clean clothes; I can imagine I was beginning to smell rank.

The surgeon has now been to see me to let me know how Fiona's operation went. Apparently the foetal distress was caused by damage to her uterus, and when they performed the emergency caesarian section they had a look to see how bad the damage was. I am sad to say for my wife that her injuries were so severe that the only course of action possible was a hysterectomy, which of course means that, in future, Neef has no chance of having any children with a future partner – so Posh and Becks are the only two she will have. There was also damage to her spleen which necessitated its removal as well. She's up in the Intensive Care Department at the moment, but they assure me that it is purely a preventative measure and, even though she has not regained consciousness, there isn't any reason why she shouldn't make a full recovery.

I am, however, not counting my chickens as my luck hasn't been the best of late. Therefore I wonder if I might ask you and James a question. Again I apologise if it sounds previous but this dilemma has been spinning round my head. In the event that Fiona doesn't survive the crash, I wondered if, after my death, James and you would take over guardianship for the twins? I realise that it is not the kind of thing that would elicit an immediate answer, but I know that you are a great mum and James is a fine stepdad to

Ellen, Lizzy and Peter and if, and it's a big if, the two newest recruits to the Robbins family could grow up in a loving environment with their half-sisters and half-brother that would gladden my heart like you wouldn't believe.

Of course I hope that this isn't necessary, as I am hoping that my darling Fiona will wake soon. If, though, she does not, and James and you agree, I will make the necessary changes to my will immediately, and will make special financial provision for the twins as well as everyone else. In the meantime, though, would it be possible to keep this request just between ourselves?

I hope to hear from you soon, and please give my love to the kids and tell them Mr Silly will come over soon.

Peter

Resolution

The waiting seemed endless, and I was getting stir crazy in the hospital. I gave the nurses my mobile number and walked slowly down the hill to get some sea air in my lungs. I walked along the promenade past the conference centre and then along the Palace Pier. I know it's now called Brighton Pier, but I grew up when there were two piers, the Palace and the West Pier, and can remember that day in the early 1970s when the West Pier caught fire, so I still call the remaining one the Palace Pier. I resisted the temptations of the giant helter skelter and the rest of the funfair and simply stood, stood there at the end and rested on the iron handrail, looking out to the vast expanse of the English Channel ahead of me, which looked a particularly shitty brown colour on this winter's day.

My phone vibrated and I thought for an instant that it was the hospital, but it wasn't. It was a text from Alice asking me if I was okay. It then vibrated again. This time it was a text from Alex, in reply to my letter. The text read 'Yes, of course, but that isn't going to happen, is it? Much love, Al and James xx'.

I smiled cautiously to myself, as the one thing I needed was the optimism of my ex-wife. A single solitary tear rolled down my cheek.

I stood there for what must have been two hours. The sun started to disappear in the west behind the downs. Nothing in particular went through my head at that time, which was a pleasant relief, as I had been contemplating the worst and every possible eventuality for what seemed like an eternity. My phone vibrated again and I answered the call. Well, when I say answered I was so flustered after hours of peace and solitude that I dropped the phone into the bloody English Channel. I took this, though, as a sign to get my arse back up to the hospital, just in case it was the medical team on the phone.

When you are physically fit, the walk from the Palace Pier to the Royal Sussex County Hospital is about ten minutes, but for a terminally ill man it takes about twice as long to walk along Madeira Drive and up Paston Place. I eventually got to where I had to be, although I was red-faced and wheezing when I got there.

"Mr Robbins, we have been trying to call you!"

"I'm sorry; I dropped my sodding phone in the sea, what's wrong?"

"Will you come with me please?"

I was taken this time not to the Families Room, but to the High Dependency Unit. The silence of the nurse filled me with dread. What was I going to find? Would my darling Neef, the woman whom I had been so distressed about leaving, leave me before I left her? I was taken through the necessary hygienic checks to make sure I wasn't carrying any infections, and then stepped into the Unit. I opened the door to Neef's room.

"Hey, Eeyore, you been out gallivanting?" I rushed to Neef and kissed her forehead with such tenderness and passion – well as much passion as you can muster in the midst of the National Health Service. Tears of joy rolled down my cheeks.

"Neef, I am so pleased to see you. I thought I'd lost you," I spluttered through the sobbing.

"I wasn't going to go anywhere, was I? Sure, I will still want to get my fair share of passionate nights courtesy of you!" She winked at me. Even though she was wired up to a drip and a monitor, it was almost as if nothing had happened.

"Have the doctors told you what they had to do?" I asked. I needn't have worried. Neef nodded.

"Sure, it's a bit emptier down there but I wasn't planning on becoming a brood mare. Posh and Becks are more than enough, and I don't even want to contemplate future relationships. As far as I am concerned I am your wife, and will always be so. At present, at least. Have you seen the babies?"

"They are beautiful, just like you. Posh is the spitting image of you, even down to the red hair!"

"Ah well, that sorts out birthday presents then – lots of bottles of Factor Fifty!"

"So what are we going to call them?"

"Well, let's think about that, although I like the idea of Hope for our daughter."

"Or Felicity!"

"Or Felicity, indeed! That gives us a shortlist of two. Hope Felicity Robbins or Felicity Hope Robbins."

"Agreed!" I kissed Fiona once more. To name our daughter after our aspirations for the future or fortuitous circumstance seemed more than appropriate.

But what about young fellow me lad, we wondered. Fiona suggested my middle name, but I was not so sure, as I always found it a little old-fashioned and wasn't sure how a boy growing up in the twenty-first century would cope being saddled with it.

"Aww, Eeyore, I quite like it and it's the best chance we have to name him after his daddy as Peter has already been allocated for your eldest son."

I promised I would think about it.

Paperwork

Feck me, what a traumatic two weeks it has been. My darling Eeyore hasn't left my side. Well, when I say he hasn't left my side, he did give me a little bit of privacy for the call of nature. I can safely say, though, that I have never felt so loved in all my life. To know that someone wills you to be well, and loves you with every fibre of his being, is such an intense, yet comforting thing to be in possession of. I feel as if I have been wrenched around in a fecking tumble dryer, but I am getting stronger as each day passes, as are the children.

When I think of the beautiful little creatures that Peter and I have created between us I just well up with tears. They are so delicate, but just so perfect little people. As soon as I was fit enough to leave my room, Peter wheeled me up to the Neo-Natal Care Unit to see them. We entered so quietly, and I remember instinctively reaching up my right hand to Peter, who took it in his own and gave it such a warm, gentle squeeze – a squeeze that told me he loved me, if I didn't know that already.

We used the services of a registrar as soon as possible to give these little bundles of loveliness official names. As we still hadn't reached a firm agreement on what names to use, we agreed to name one child each, with no, and that was promised, no argument from the other partner. We tossed a coin and I got to name Becks.

As Posh was the first one out officially, by about forty-five seconds, Peter went first. My breath was taken away when he said 'Felicity Hope Fiona Robbins'. The fecking git! He gave no sign that he was going to add a third name.

And so the time came for me to officially name Becks. I took a deep breath and gave his names to the registrar.

"Dylan Maurice Robbins"

Peter looked at me, stunned by my choice but ultimately approving. I explained later that I agreed in part with him about his middle name, Maurice, but I didn't want to lose it altogether. As for the Dylan, well, Eeyore was always stunned by my DMs and, by choosing a name beginning with 'D', I'd always have a memento of that particular nugget. Choosing a name beginning with D was simple, I went for my favourite singer, or favourite character from 'The Magic Roundabout', whichever way you choose to look at it.

Hopefully I'll be out of hospital soon, as I want to spend some quality time with Eeyore, Felicity and Dylan. I mustn't forget my darling Seamus, I never would, but I am aware there are a limited number of days ahead of us together as a family.

Before anyone says anything, Peter told me that, while he was fretting when I was unconscious, he chose to send his ex-wife a letter, asking her to take care of Felicity and Dylan if I didn't survive. I must admit I was taken aback at first, not totally due to the nature of the request, but because I didn't realise I was actually in that much danger. Thinking about it now, it seems like a very sensible request as she is a very good mum to Peter's other three children, who we really must get over and see sometime. I mean, they haven't met their new brother and sister yet!

Part Three – The Hereafter

The Last Will and Testament of Peter Maurice Robbins

I would like to point out straight away that this isn't an actual will. It's just that, with a limited number of days ahead of me, I need to put some thoughts down before I become too weak. I weighed myself today, and I am now only six stones in weight. It's surely not long before I have to leave Fiona, Seamus and the kids, but I need to get my thoughts down on paper before I do.

First of all I need to address my mum, sister, brother and my nieces. I am sorry that I haven't been all I could have been over the years. I know I am a grumpy old tosspot and am sometimes hard to get along with, but I am genuinely sorry, and wish that I could spend more time with you. It's only when you know there's a literal deadline that you value things more.

Next it is the turn of my ex-wife, Alex. Thank you. I actually need to thank you for two things. Firstly a big thank you for having three wonderful children with me. Ellen, Lizzy and Peter are three of the best things that I have ever done. I know that, with your and James' guidance and love, plus the love of their step-mum, half-sister and half-brother, they will continue to grow to become fully worthwhile members of the world, who know the value of compassion, understanding, tolerance, friendship and, above all, love. Thank you as well for leaving me all those years ago. This may sound strange, but if you think about it, without our divorce, I never would have met Fiona, or had Felicity and Dylan.

To Ellen, well, what can I say to my big girl? I am so, so proud of the woman you are becoming. Your personality has warmth, honesty and you always think of others. You have made your old dad so proud. Now go ahead and forge your own path in the world, and be good to yourself, and all those about whom you care.

Right, Lizzy, this is Mr Silly speaking. I know that you are not one for showing feelings on the outside, but I also know that inside there is a sensitive girl who wants to be loved and looked after as well as she deserves, and believe me, you deserve a lot. I don't have favourites, but you have made me smile so much with all your wit and humour. Never stop making people smile, my darling, and you won't go far wrong.

Now, Peter, young man. First of all sorry for surrounding you with sisters. They will love you like their lives depended on it. I will love you forever, and I know that you will command respect wherever you go, purely because you are so sensitive and thoughtful. Stay that way please, my darling boy.

Felicity and Dylan, you have only just entered my world, but I want you to know that I will love you always. Your dad was a man who sometimes forgot what was important in this world, but I want you to remember one thing – your mum came into my life at a very dark time, and she brought such light, energy and love into it that I have no regrets whatsoever, apart from the fact that it saddens me that I will not see you grow up. Your daddy loves you.

And finally to you, my darling Neef. You are about to undergo something that I wouldn't wish on you, but I know you wouldn't have it any other way. It's only by nearly losing you a couple of weeks back that I realised how much I love you. Thank you, and thanks to Seamus, for coming into my life. Thank you for helping me to create and thank you for giving birth to Felicity and Dylan, who are so lovely that they equal my earlier greatest achievements, Ellen, Lizzy and Peter. I know that you will shower enough love and affection on them for both of us put together. I am about to enter a stage of my illness where I may eventually become incoherent and speak drivel. When I say that, I mean more drivel than I usually utter. Never forget that, even if I am in the ultimate stages of my cancer, I will never stop loving you. Never forget me, please.

I will sign off now, but I want this to be heard. I am not ready to go. I will hang around until the last bloody minute. You hear me? I will not go!

John Denver

March 18th 2012

It seems strange, but you do really know when the end is nigh. Don't worry, that previous part of my journal is locked away and sealed in an envelope. I couldn't tell if it was too maudlin or not.

Today I reduced my darling Neef to tears. We were sitting in the living room, just relaxing after a game of 'change the nappy', and all I said to her was 'you know I want to be cremated, don't you?' I am sorry if it seemed like the wrong moment, but I am at the stage of my illness when, if something occurs to me, I blurt it out immediately so that I don't forget, particularly as the morphine is making me swim away into the land of Oz from time to time.

Neef wasn't angry, she understood, but it, all of these, my illness, our relationship, the children, are all so jumbled together in such an exquisitely tragic mess that I sometimes struggle to get my head around it.

The twins are wonderful, I can hold them each in one forearm, and they are so bonny. Ah, bonny, I hate that word! Anyway, we hadn't had a portrait in a while, so Neef took advantage of me holding both my children to do what will probably be one, final sketch. She showed this one to me, and it brought such joy, as well as so many tears, to my eyes. This encapsulated everything about my situation – a man nearing the end of his life holding the two small infants that represent his future, that last remnant of his spirit that will surely live on forever.

My friend Dr Matthews came to visit me at home today. He examined me and then sat with a cup of coffee to chat to me.

"Peter, you know what I am going to say, don't you?"

"I probably do, but I still want to hear you say it, and then there is no chance of me denying it to myself."

"Well, you aren't going to improve much from the present. The pain, if anything, will get worse, and you will get progressively weaker and be able to do fewer things for yourself."

"So what exactly are you saying?"

"Ok, you old bastard, what I am saying is that maybe now is the time for you to take up that room in the horse piss." It's okay, horse piss was a private joke between the three of us. Basically, Dr Matthews thought it was now the time to enter my 'end of life' plans. This didn't mean insurance or anything, but simply what I and Neef had agreed to do when the time came. We agreed that I would go into a hospice, to ease the burden on her, to have my pain managed more systematically and, when the time came, I could meet my end knowing that my loved ones were around me, knowing I was at peace. In one, final bid to add a sense of the absurd, Lizzy, Fiona and I agreed that, at the time of my death, there should be music. Not sad music, no dirges, as there was so much for which to be thankful. No, they would play 'Going Underground' by The Jam.

After Dr Matthews had gone, Neef put on the radio. It was the crappiest timing of all, and we just held each other and wept. The song that came on was by John Denver, and the song itself was 'Leaving on a Jet-Plane'.

Valediction

March 23rd 2012

I have decided that this is going to be the final entry into my own version of 'chronicle of a death foretold'. I've been in the hospice for three days now, and they are all being very nice to me. Nothing is too much trouble, although I hate being a burden on anyone. My abdominal pain is now so intense that there are only very short periods when I am lucid enough to indulge in rational conversation, or even type. This journal entry is being scribbled down on paper with a pencil, and a very nice lady by the name of Valerie is going to type it up for me overnight. See? As I said, nothing is too much trouble here.

Yesterday I had a visit from Alex, James and the kids. Lizzy took great delight in reading me some Spike Milligan poetry as we both delight in absurdity. Ellen was calm and composed, and Peter was very quiet. I think he is still struggling to come to terms with the fact that his dad will die very soon, and when the time come for him to go he gave me the biggest hug ever. In fact, if I come to think of it, hugs are the thing I will miss the most after I have gone. Then again, that's ridiculous, as I won't actually be in a position to miss anything. Let's just say that the moment I die I want to imagine myself in the arms of the woman I love.

My biggest comfort at the moment is music. Not the absurd music that Lizzy and I delight in listening to, but comforting, homely music that has real meaning. Mellowing out to mellow music gives me a chance to occasionally veg out and it takes my mind off the pain. I am never alone. Even though she has Felicity and Dylan to look after, my beloved Neef spends as much time as possible here, talking to me, holding me, crying with me, or just being there, a physical presence near me as my journey reaches its end.

The whole idea of a journey is weird, but it seems appropriate, I think. Ever since that Sunday last year, when I first noticed the pain in my abdomen, right through to that day on Beachy Head, when I met my beloved Neef, through my treatment, marriage, the birth of the twins, even that sodding car crash, it has been one mad adventure and, you know what, I am not sure I would miss a thing. Well, I'd be happy to have opted out of the car crash, but there we go.

My role in that great performance that they call life will soon draw to its close. In fact, these will be my final words on the subject. It's not that I intend to die soon, but the curtain is due to close on my life pretty soon. As the sands of my own particular egg-timer are running very low (and I apologise profusely for using all these bloody meaningless metaphors and clichés in one journal entry), I would like to use the remaining strength I have to spend more time with my darling Fiona, and my five wonderful children.

This journal has been an odd companion over my illness, but it has allowed me to record my thoughts. Whoever reads it in the future, I am so bloody sorry about the bloody swearing.

I am not a religious man, but please God, just grant me a few days more.

Valediction – Part Two

First of all I must apologise for the absence of entries into Peter's journal, but it's been a traumatic kind of week. Well, to be honest, traumatic is a bit of an understatement. We have, all of us, just about recovered enough of our composure to make sense of the events of the last week.

As you might have realised, the man I love, my dearest, sweetest, most darling Eeyore, is no longer with us. He is now at rest and at peace and in no pain, but it makes no difference, I still miss him like no pain I have ever felt before. I am simultaneously despairing, bereft and furious. Yes I am angry, and I know that it is my grief expressing itself, but I have to work through it. Everything just feels so fecking unfair at present. That will pass, I know, and a more sensible kind of grief will take over, and then in time the pain will ease.

Note there that I did not say that the pain will go. I know I will miss Eeyore and will hurt because of it in my heart until the day I die. What will happen, though, is that I will develop coping strategies, so that the occasions of real, intense pain will become shorter and more infrequent.

There are some very strange things happening, though, and they are not at all pleasant. Ever since Peter died I have been physically unable to remember him how he was before he became really ill and really thin. I know it's the grief doing its fecking weird work, but I hate it. I want to remember my lovely, cuddly Eeyore, not the shadow of the man who spent the last few weeks with me.

So, I suppose I had best explain what happened this last week, hadn't I, in order to make this journal as complete as possible.

Peter's last journal entry was on Friday 23rd, and we made the next two days as happy as we possibly could. Saturday saw a huge family gathering at the hospice – nothing was too much trouble and they didn't mind the whole family descending. Sheila, his mum, his sister and her family, and his brother, even dear, sweet little old Auntie Maud from Burgess Hill came down for what we decided was going to be a party.

Eeyore and I both decided that there was no point in being morose waiting for the dreaded moment to come. Alex and James were there, along with Peter's three lovely children, and I sprang a surprise on them all by bringing Felicity and Dylan along to spend a little bit of time with their daddy. We drank a glass of wine and chatted as if it was just your average run-of-the-mill celebration. Eeyore was in his element, and for a little while it appeared as if the stresses and strains of his illness were long gone. At the end of the day everyone tried to avoid tears, and to just say farewell as you do when you expect to see someone very soon.

The one thing that really choked me up was when Eeyore shook poor young Peter's hand and wished him 'all the best' – it was like the passing on of a flame, like some kind of family relay, as if my darling Eeyore was signing off from being head of the family and leaving his young son in charge of a bevy of females.

Saturday night was so sweet, and so sad. Peter kissed the babies and appeared to whisper something in their ears, at least I couldn't make out what he said. As I said goodbye to him I gave him a huge kiss and a lingering hug, and all he said to me was 'never forget'. I think he knew that his time was nearly up.

When I returned the next day, he was in a coma, and slowly making his way to his eternal reward. The only upsetting thing was that apparently he called out my name in the night, and it will upset me for many years to come that I could not be there, but I had to look after the twins.

Sunday was a day of peace and restfulness. Peter was unconscious and so I did not go in for brass bands and fireworks, I just played the radio and chatted to him as if things were as normal as they could be. The hospice staff came in at regular intervals to make sure that he was comfortable – they are so lovely – and they made sure I had food and drink.

At a little before 10pm two hospice nurses came in to check on us, and to turn Eeyore so he had a comfortable night. I took this opportunity to nip to the loo, as I knew he wouldn't be alone. When I came back, the head nurse was waiting for me.

"Mrs Robbins, I am very sorry, but your husband has gone."

The fecking bastard! He knew I would hang around by his side, so he took advantage of my call of nature to depart. That said, how could I be angry with my darling at that moment. He had finally reached the point where he had no pain, and was at peace. I walked to the MP3 player attached to the radio and put on the song appointed for this moment.

A tear rolled down my face, a single solitary glassy tear. I walked slowly over to him, bent over him and kissed him for the last time. 'So long, my darling Eeyore' were the words I said I think. I then added the traditional Celtic blessing 'May the road rise up to meet you and the wind be at your back'.

Peter was moved to the Chapel and I rang James, Alex's husband, who had kindly brought me over and told me to ring him if I needed picking up. He did so, and he very kindly said to me that he would pick me up the next day so the three of us, Alex,

James and I, could break the sad news to the children that their daddy was gone.

The children knew what was happening. I think they must have a sixth sense about these things. I arrived at the house in Ticehurst with the twins in tow. I know it sounds strange but I wanted them close by as much as possible, as if that part of Peter that was in them would keep me company during this tough task. I entered the house and Alex called the children down from upstairs. They did not rush, but were very happy to see their brother and sister in their car seats. We all went and sat in the living room.

I didn't have to say anything. Ellen broke the silence.

"Dad's gone, hasn't he?"

"Yes, Ellen, I am afraid he has." I was not the only one who had difficulty coping with the news as the tears rolled down my face. Ellen walked over to me and gave me an enormous hug, the kind of hug that said 'shhh, it's okay, it's going to be fine'; she then looked at me, gave me a kiss on the cheek and then kissed the twins.

Peter was next. He was silent. I am not sure whether things had sunk in but I am worldly enough to know that you don't force people to confront their grief – it comes out soon enough. He came and gave me a hug, then crouched down and started talking in such a sweet 'talking to infants' way to Felicity and Dylan.

There were huge, enormous, beach ball-sized tears rolling down darling Lizzy's face. She sobbed openly and Alex put her arm round her youngest daughter.

"So Mr Silly has gone off to be silly in heaven, I s'pose,"

"Yes, darling, he has" was all I could muster in reply.

"Well, St Peter had better watch out for a whoopee cushion at the Pearly Gates, then!" She ran over to me and gave me an enormous, wet, sobbing hug, and then we all cried. After that we dried our eyes and then tried to speak of the happy memories we had of Peter, the silliness, the affection, the love. Alex and James very kindly made some lunch but we were none of us very hungry. After lunch James took me and the twins home, as I felt the need to be home amongst my memories in the house that Eeyore and I shared for such a brief, but intensely happy time.

A couple of days later I was mooching around the house, opening the post, which contained numerous cards of condolence. Among all the stuff coming through the letterbox was a padded envelope from Ticehurst: A covering note from Alex expressed the hope that I was bearing up as well as could be expected, and that she hoped I didn't mind, but the children had each written a letter to their dad to go in this journal. I sat down, agape with astonishment at such a lovely, sweet gesture by Ellen, Lizzy and Peter. As this was their daddy's journal, a chronicle of his illness and log of the events of his death, how could I refuse?

Farewells

Here are the letters that the children wrote to their dad.

From Peter

Daddy,

I am not too sure what to write. This is a very sad time for all of us, because you have gone to heaven to be at peace. I am very proud to have had you as my daddy. I know I am quiet, but that does not mean that I do not listen.

All I can say is that if I can be half the man you were, then I won't go far wrong. I will never forget you, and will never forget what you told me in the hospice at your party.

I miss you, and always will

Peter xxxxx

From Lizzy

Mr Silly,

Well, I suppose you are having a fine old time now, aren't you? All that free beer in the Paradise Arms, being able to chat to all the people you know and, above all, lots of silliness!

Seriously, though, I really miss you already, and to know that I will never be able to speak to you again fills my heart with so many tears. Maybe the pain will ease with time, but at the moment I am not sure I want it to. If it does then I might think you will turn up on the doorstep to blow a raspberry on my cheek.

I am not sure what to write, but will remember one of your cricketing poems:

And when the one great scorer comes

to write against your name,

He marks not whether you won or lost,

But whether you called the umpire 'Stumpy'!

I will always love you, Mr Silly

Lizzy xxxxx

Ellen's letter is next. I was taken aback by it, then realized the sentiment was from a song in 'La Cage aux Folles', which she had been rehearsing for at school.

From Ellen

Dad

I have wanted to sing 'The Best of Times' to you as it has meant everything to me over the last few weeks. I was dreading the day when you left me. I have been saying the words to myself over and over and over again. One thing's for sure, I will never forget my unforgotten yesterdays!

I promise I will make you proud of me.

I miss you, dad, and always will. Sleep on, until I see you again.

Ellen xxxxxxxxxxxxxxx

The Last Farewell

I could have easily included the lyrics of a song by Roger Whittaker in this journal. It's something I hadn't heard before, but I found it on Peter's MP3 player. I listened to it, and the chorus brought tears to my eyes. It was called 'The Last Farewell'.

Of course I was now sobbing, but these words stuck with me so much. I decided that these three lines of a song from forty years ago would be the text for my wreath to my beloved Eeyore at his funeral.

Ah, the funeral. I was fortunate that Peter had had the foresight to make all the necessary arrangements himself, particularly as I was busying myself with Felicity and Dylan. All I had to do was organise the date at the crematorium. There wasn't much of a delay, so the time was booked at 3pm on Monday 2nd April. Peter had decided that he didn't want a church service followed by a trip to the crematorium, so he opted for one single service. It wasn't going to be overly religious, but there would be a hymn, a reading and a prayer from the presiding priest, and a eulogy.

The priest came to see me a few days before and asked me what hymn Peter had chosen. I didn't know it, but he had apparently chosen 'the family funeral hymn', a delightfully titled song called 'The Old Rugged Cross'. Now, even though I was not aware of it, I would not deny my darling husband his choices, so that was that. The entrance and exit music were also chosen. The coffin would enter the chapel to the Largo from Dvorak's 'New World Symphony', which was the basis of the song 'Going Home', written by Williams Arms Fisher. How fitting, I thought.

The priest also asked me about what I was going to say in my eulogy to my deceased husband. I am afraid that my answer to that question was 'oh feck!' I hadn't realised that I would be asked to deliver it, and now I had three days to prepare! This would require some thought, some thought by a recently-widowed young woman who is coming to terms with her grief whilst looking after two small babies.

Well, the day came, and the hearses carried me, Sheila, and the children to the crematorium. Everyone was solemn, and it was so lovely to see a large gathering there who had come to pay their respects to my lovely man. Just as at our wedding a few months ago, everybody wore a dark purple lapel ribbon. We entered solemnly and quietly, and the music by Dvorak was just lovely. The priest gave his address, and then we sang the hymn which, although old, was beautiful when sung by a congregation wanting to pay its respects. Then I gave my eulogy, which I will include in full a little later. After that we had the prayers, and my darling's coffin slowly disappeared behind the curtain. As it faded from view, I murmured 'bye bye, my lovely Eeyore, I won't forget!' The final blessing was given and then, in a break from tradition, we sang as we left the chapel. It was a song about Eeyore's adopted home county, 'Sussex by the Sea'. It seemed so jolly and uplifting and brought some joy to our hearts on this cold day, although the line about 'all the girls we left behind' was heartbreaking for me.

From the chapel we adjourned to our house in Winchelsea Beach, for the wake. This, I decided, should not be a sad occasion at all. It was very much time to celebrate and remember the good times, to eat, drink, and have happy memories. At the end of the evening I kissed everyone goodbye and settled down to a quiet evening on my own, with my children and my memories, a glass of Bushmills and a tear in my eye.

Eulogy

Beidh muid rudaí cosúil arís 's fheiceáil – We will never see his like again.

What can I tell you about Peter Maurice Robbins that you don't know already? Well, I dare say that you have all known my darling Eeyore longer than I have, yet I, as his widow, have been asked to deliver the eulogy. I sincerely hope that I do justice to my darling man and the trust that you have put in me.

I would talk of a man with an infinite capacity to love those around him, a darling son, brother, uncle, nephew, a fantastic daddy to five beautiful children, and the most fantastic husband I could ever have dreamed to have.

I asked a few members of the family, both in-laws and out-laws, for some words that would sum Peter up, and here is the list I have collated – patient, reliable, loving, very silly (thanks Lizzy!), intolerant of injustice, placid, beer-loving, cricketing, and bald.

There are so many things for which I am grateful to Peter. He introduced me to his family, from his mum, his brother and sister, his Auntie Maud but, above all, to his children. Knowing that I have these three amazing young people in my life is helping me through these dark days. I must also add that the company of our own two children, my darling twins, Felicity and Dylan, is a huge comfort. I would charge every one of you to remind both of them of the special man who was their daddy when you see them when they are older.

I hope you will appreciate that a lot of the memories that I shared with my darling Peter are private. We went through a lot, to say the least. Diagnosis of a terminal illness, love, laughs, near-tragedy, and it all led to this, me standing here trying ever so hard to be strong.

I will treasure every memory of every moment that Peter and I spent together. He was a very special man and I was privileged that he shared his love with me. His love was truly a gift and we are all so, so lucky to have been on the receiving end of that gift, aren't we?

I have received many cards from so many lovely people to tell me how high the esteem was in which Peter was held, but I would like to end this eulogy with the sentiments expressed in a song that means a lot to me. I think it sums it all up, here in this chapel, on this very sad day.

If I paint a picture

How would you, have me paint it?

In a room, with a view,

With me standing next to you?

You'd hold my hand again

Smiling through the pain

The sun shining through the rain

And the paint that covers all the cracks

Would stop the hurt from ever coming back

If I try, and you try too,

Then we will be

All we were meant to be

And nobody will see through the glue

Except me and you.

Back to a place in time

Where memories are so sublime

'Cos our lives were so simple and,

My soulmate and my best friend.

But time changes many things,

And life brings what life will bring

And I think perhaps

I should stop looking back

'Cos I break each time I try

To fill the gaps.

If I try, and you try too

Then we will be

All we were meant to be

And nobody will see through the glue

Except me and you.

Thank you for listening, and for coming here today to show how much you thought of Peter.

Moving on

So here I am, the Widow Robbins, living here out by the sea with my two young children, who are now five months old and have just entered that wondrous stage in their development that is called teething.

Sleepless nights, shitty nappies and now this! Peter, you knew about this all, didn't you?

The last couple of months have not been the best, but I guess you didn't have to be clairvoyant to see that. I should chronicle everything so that this journal reaches its end as complete as it can be.

The first month after Peter's death was so traumatic. I suddenly felt so isolated, so abandoned and so, so alone. My grief was intense, it still is I guess, but things are slowly easing, just a little bit. Easter weekend was nice, well as nice as it could be under the circumstances. I was invited over to Ticehurst to join in with Easter egg hunts and roast dinner with Alex, James and the children. We were all a little subdued, but that is not to say that we were morose. Peter was quiet, but seemed to be coping well with the fact that he had lost his father at a very young age. Ellen had grown up, I thought, and was being so strong for her brother and sister. Lizzy took my breath away again when she insisted on calling me 'Mrs Silly'. At first it was very strange and not a little upsetting, but then I reasoned that this young lady saw what it was in me that attracted her father, and saw that similar outlook on life living on in me and, I dearly hope, in the twins.

When I got home, though, the silence and remoteness was even more palpable. I am so sorry to be writing about the next events. Alice and Norman had kindly offered to give me a break from being a full-time widow and mother, and came down to pick up the children for a couple of nights. Even though I was grateful for their kind gesture, after they had gone the loneliness increased ten-fold.

That night, the solitude was so intense, that I put my special 'misery playlist' on the MP3 player and I had the sound of The Beach Boys, Pink Floyd and yes, dear old Roger Whittaker to keep me company. I opened the drinks cabinet, where I would find a prized bottle of Jameson's Whiskey. I opened the bottle and, for want of a better phrase, I climbed inside.

As the effects of the alcohol started to take hold of my system, I wobbled to the bathroom cabinet and had a look to see what I could find. In there was a packet of paracetamol tablets that I had subconsciously safeguarded for this eventuality.

I poured another glass of whiskey and laid the tablets out in front of me. Fifteen tablets, in a neat pyramid pattern. Now all I had to do was take them. If I managed this, I would fall asleep with more alcohol inside me and would soon join my beloved Eeyore forever.

And then I woke up! 'Oh feck', I thought, 'you can't even do that fecking properly!' I was lying on the sofa with a duvet covering me. I was fully-clothed and I rapidly realised that I had the makings of a killer hangover! A sick-bucket was conveniently placed by my side and, lo and behold, it appeared that it had been made use of during the night! I tried to raise my head from the sofa but, the moment that I did, I felt the compelling urge to place my gaping mouth over the bucket again.

Eventually, after what felt like turning my stomach inside out, I felt strong enough to get up. I walked gingerly into the dining-room and found a light breakfast laid out for me – toast, marmalade, orange juice and hot coffee. Beside the cafetière was an old-style medicine bottle which, upon closer inspection, contained the fifteen paracetamol tablets I had carefully laid out on the table in front of me the night before when I was at my lowest ebb.

Between the coffee and the medicine bottle was a letter, which sat in an opened envelope.

Unexpected Letters

Winchelsea Beach, November 2011

Adam,

It isn't all that often that your big brother takes time out to get in touch with you, is it? I know I haven't been around for you, to offer advice or do your bookkeeping and all the assorted things like that, and for that I am truly sorry.

To be honest I am in awe of my kid brother. I went to university in Surrey to study accountancy, not studying English at the University of Exeter like you. I don't begrudge you it one bit, as I was never one for reading Chaucer or Tennyson. I am so proud that you achieved your ambition to be a professional author, and hope that you continue to write best-sellers for years to come!

Even though I haven't called on you as much as I should, I need you to do me a favour, little brother. It's nearing the end of 2011 and I am nearing the end of my life. There's no point me putting a gloss on it, as we both know what lies ahead for me. I am very lucky to be husband to a wonderful woman, and father to two beautiful and very cute little people. I am not trying to exaggerate my importance to the female gender (last of the lukewarm lovers, that's me), but I can imagine that, after all I have put Neef through, she will need keeping an eye on from time to time to make sure she doesn't get too lonely.

I know you will do this one small thing for me, as in essence I know you are a good kid, even if you are soon going to be forty. I'd prefer you to let Neef know when you are dropping in, but feel free to visit anytime. I enclose a front door key for your convenience.

When you do visit, please do give her my love and tell her I am still by her side.

Take care of her and the kids, mate, and look after yourself

Peter

Mr Robbins

"I must say it's good to see my sister-in-law up and about", said Adam as he came through the front door. He'd taken advantage of me sleeping off half a bottle of whiskey to take poor old Seamus out for a walk.

That poor fecking dog – I know I have neglected him of late. I have been so caught up in my grief and caring for the twins that he has been at the back of my thoughts. I walked over to him and gave the soppy old chap a huge hug.

"It's good to see you too, Adam," I gave him a quick hug and a peck on the cheek, "thank you for sorting me out last night."

"Hey, let's not go into that, and let's not talk about it. Put it down to experience."

"Thanks, Adam. I don't make a habit of trying to..."

"I said let's not talk about it."

I nodded, and sat down to eat the rest of my breakfast. The streaks of springtime sunlight sparkled through the dining-room window and today didn't seem half as bleak as last night did. I had only met Adam briefly at mine and Peter's wedding, and was so caught up in the joys of the day that I hadn't had the chance to get to know him properly. He was so kind today – nothing would be made of or mentioned about last night, whereas he could have been leaping about making a fuss. I didn't even know that he was an author until I read the letter! An idea occurred to me, and I pondered it with a coffee mug perched a centimetre from my mouth.

"Adam, don't take this the wrong way, but I'd like to make you a proposition."

"Oooh, I'm all ears – must take after my dad. What did you have in mind?"

I explained that, throughout the course of his illness, my beloved Eeyore had kept a journal to chronicle his illness, record thoughts and feelings and any minor events that might crop up. Well, I suggested that, if Adam could make sense of the records, writings and jottings that my late husband had made, I could sort out the numerous pencil sketches that I had made of Peter during our time together.

Adam was happy to help. He'd just published his third novel, and was pondering a change in career. He'd been accepted for a postgraduate teacher training course in Brighton next September, so would have a bit of time on his hands until then. He hadn't got a family – he'd got an on-off girlfriend up in Chislehurst and would visit her from time to time, but would be around as much or as little as I wanted him to. He added this would also give him the perfect opportunity to spend time with his sister-in-law, niece and nephew and get to know the three of us a little better. Like any good author he suggested days out so we could talk about Eeyore so he could get a better idea of my relationship with him to help him make more sense of the journal. A fecking perfect idea, I thought, and a bit of company for me and the children.

Adam, had to zip back to Chislehurst to see Claudia, who hailed from Bremen, but said he'd be back the next day. He had an idea, and pulled out his mobile phone, which he proceeded to drop on the floor. He bent down and picked it up.

"Just going to give Alice a bell," he explained. He dialled her number and waited for her to answer.

"Hello sis! I know, long time no speak and all that. Look, I have been down on the coast visiting Fiona and the dog... why? Because our bloody brother asked me to, that's why! Anyway, I'm back off home tonight but Fiona has asked me to help her make sense of Peter's journal jottings, so I will be back down tomorrow afternoon. Do you want me to pick up the twins and bring them down for you? What do you mean, is my car big enough? It's a sodding people carrier! Right then, see you at two o'clock tomorrow afternoon. Say hello to Norman and the girls for me."

He rang off, put the phone back in his pocket, looked at me, smiled and said "sorted!"

What a breath of fresh air he was! Nothing like my darling Peter, of course. Adam had an almost bohemian air and a faded corduroy jacket. I noticed that it had leather elbow patches.

"Not going to be a geography teacher, are you?"

"Oh, the patches!" Adam laughed, a deep hearty laugh. "Nope. Believe it or not I am going to train to be an English teacher. Fortunately I don't think the kids will be studying the kinds of things I write – I mainly write mild erotica for fifty-something bored wives!" I snorted as I imagined what Peter would have made of the subject matter of his brother's writing.

Adam asked me if I was going to be okay, and I explained that I would be fine. He got his stuff together, said goodbye to Seamus and put it into the back of his car. He waved as his battered Chrysler Voyager left the drive.

Records

The next day, I decided to set about tackling the heap of detritus that prevented my home at Winchelsea Beach from looking anywhere near its best. There was a pile of washing up to negotiate, and I was delighted to get through it with only a couple of breakages. The next challenge in my domestic assault course was a pile of laundry – my wardrobe was extensive and therefore I allowed myself the 'luxury' of leaving my washing until the very last minute. It was all very new to me, as my status of domestic goddess was taken away from me the moment Peter rumbled that I couldn't even separate a darks from a whites wash, which I suspect was the moment he first set foot inside my flat in Eastbourne and he noticed my grey knickers on the radiator.

The house was looking immaculate when the Chrysler rolled up onto the drive, I opened the door and rushed to the car, where I opened the rear door and saw my darlings. It was really strange, but I felt as if I had been away from Felicity and Dylan for weeks. Then again, my brush with doing something stupid seemed to have brought the 'heavy' stage of my grief to an end, and so it could be said that I had come back to my babies properly for the first time in weeks.

Adam gave me a smile and a cheeky 'hello, sis'. He had obviously been warned by my late husband about my lack of cooking ability as he had brought the makings of a delightful dinner – trout, potatoes, broccoli and the ingredients for a sauce accompaniment. He pulled a bottle of Beaujolais out of the wine rack and put it in the fridge to chill. He then fished around in his bag and told me to sit down.

"Right, Mrs Robbins, I've been scratching my head over the last twenty-four hours. I got a splinter in my finger as a result, but I set my mind to this book we are going to come up with. I brought my digital camera with me. I was wondering if it needed a sort of upbeat ending, with photographs of you and the twins, and Ellen, Peter and Lizzy, so anyone who reads it doesn't end up wanting to see the bottom of Beachy Head when they get to the end."

I couldn't help but agree, but insisted that we shouldn't make the book too syrupy – it had to contain all the highs and lows of Peter's illness – from our glorious wedding day to the car crash, from the moment Peter and I first slept together to my attempted suicide, if you can call it that. It must be the whole journey, not just edited highlights, as I put it.

The conversation continued over dinner, and over that delicious bottle of wine. I couldn't help but listen to all the ideas that Adam had about the book. He wasn't taking over, not in the least, but he had a writer's eye with which to add suggestions. He offered the idea that the book should be split into three distinct sections, that I should include the letters and all the assorted extras that were sent, even if they caused sadness as I re-read them.

The one thing I was noticing was that the cloud of despair that had hung over me from the time of Peter's death was starting to lift. As Adam and I chatted, I think I even allowed my face to break into a smile. There was familial comfort in me chatting to my brother-in-law – sure, Adam had similarities to his brother, but there were also sufficient differences to make sure that I didn't get an eerie, spooky feeling as I did. The conversation continued through the evening, through children's bedtime and into the evening. We planned an outing for the near future, which would prove a pleasant day out, I was sure.

Getting all of Peter's journal writings together was not easy. However brilliant an accountant he may have been, sorting out all the pieces of paper upon which these thoughts, ideas, records and feelings were written, printed or scrawled proved to be a fecking huge task. The biggest problem was that there still appeared to be gaps in Peter's narrative. Now he had told me that everything was there, but maybe it was a problem with my grief and recollection that caused this mental block in my mind. Then again, it did sometimes appear that my darling Eeyore was deliberately leaving little puzzles for me to solve.

Some writings caused me to sob openly. The extract entitled 'The Last Will and Testament of Peter Maurice Robbins' was so tenderly written, and displayed so much thought that I was in floods of tears once more, and was worried that my intense grief would be back to haunt me as it had done so weeks before.

And from one moment of seeming despair there was then one of frustration at what seemed like a puzzle. It was a simple, clean, white envelope, and upon it Peter, I presume, had written the following:

F

FIL?

C DM!

P

So either there was some kind of message there, or Peter was creating a new eye chart for use in opticians' surgeries. I dare say that mystery would solve itself one day!

Openings

Well, spring turned to summer and Adam and I just about had a book ready. We looked at the sketches I had made of Peter during his illness and made a final decision as to which ones we should include. There were some definites for inclusion, but things like the sketch of Peter throwing his guts up on a cross channel ferry were scrapped and consigned to a safe forever. Photographs would also be there, including that beautiful photograph of him surrounded by all the family and, especially, all five of his children, on the day before he left us. It seemed to be a photo full of happiness, full of hope, and not full of sadness, which is how I think he would like to be remembered. Remember the man, not the Malcolm, would have been Peter's mantra.

Adam did take some pictures of me and the twins out in the rolling countryside of the Downs. Although still very young, and in spite of me being a biased mummy, I do think they are very photogenic and are always so very quiet and obedient when there is a camera around.

In late July the whole country seemed to be in a frenzy. In fact, the madness had started several weeks earlier. From the rain-soaked joy of the Diamond Jubilee celebrations to the Olympic Torch relay, the whole country seemed to be ready to party. I wasn't despairing, but wasn't exactly in the party spirit. In mid-July I received a phone call from Adam. He wasn't a happy man. It transpired that Claudia had shipped off back to Bremen, but he wasn't totally despairing about it, which was good, as I wasn't totally sure I was ready to help out the fecking broken hearts squad as I was still steadily climbing out of my own grief. Adam did, though, have a question for me.

"Oh I'll get through it, but it has left me with a gap, as it were. I had got tickets for the Opening Ceremony of the Olympics, but now have nobody to go with. If you can get someone to mind the twins, would you like to come with me?"

"Why I'd love to, Adam. Can't you find someone happier to go with, though?" I asked, as I was sure that I was still not ideal company for such a splendid occasion. After a little cheerful persuasion, though, Adam managed to convince me that I would love the whole occasion. It would mean a late night, though, and he would organise food and transport so I needn't worry about anything. I knew that Alice or Alex would be happy to look after Felicity and Dylan, so this was something to look forward to.

"That's sorted then!" said Adam, "I'll pick you up on the day at 4pm. We'll get the Tube to the stadium and will eat beforehand. See you in a week or so!"

Well, the time passed quickly and before I knew it the day had arrived. Alice and Norman had been more than happy to have the twins for the night, and came down in the morning to pick them up. Alice was very happy that morning and both she and Norman waved happily as they drove off to spend time with Felicity and Dylan. Now all I had to do was to get ready. Would I need to dress stylishly, or for comfort? What the feck did 'dress stylishly' mean for Fiona Robbins? In the end I opted for the comfortable look, particularly as I envisaged the ceremony ending very late at night when there might be a chill in the air.

Adam came down from Chislehurst and picked me up at 3pm. We drove back up to South London, and then I had my first-ever trip on the Docklands Light Railway, which was uneventful but not unpleasant. We arrived in the brand-new Olympic Park at about half past five and sat down to take in the view of the stadium and to indulge in a spot of people-watching.

"Fancy your picnic now?" Adam pulled round a wicker basket and started undoing the leather straps.

"Feck, yes! I could eat a scabby Weston donkey! What you got for us?" To be honest I hadn't eaten all day and would have wolfed down whatever Adam had brought, but what he had prepared was absolutely perfect – mini quiche Lorraine, smoked salmon blinis, a fresh summer fruit salad and a bottle of champagne. We ate ourselves silly and sat back on the grass, watching the visitors to the Park. Funnily enough, I had taken my sketch book with me, and decided to draw a view of the events on this auspicious day. I suggested that Adam should invent a back-story for different people I pointed out – the first one was an American couple who were arguing over camera settings before they entered the stadium. The 'camera settings' bit is not invented back-story, by the way, as the argument was so loud that everyone could hear.

We took our seats in the stadium and awaited the Opening Ceremony. There was music, cheering, and a clear sense of anticipation. Once the proceedings were underway, I found it totally breathtaking – the choirs, the drama, the spectacle and the comedy – it was definitely a once in a lifetime event to experience and, I thought, something that Peter would have loved to have seen. I wiped a small tear away from my eye. Adam noticed this and gave me a brotherly hug, which cheered me. To find that I had a brother, for want of a better word who was looking out for me was doing me the world of good.

As the final strains of Paul McCartney ended and we all marvelled at the firework display illuminating the night sky, Adam and I decided that we should see about getting back to the car. The DLR was packed with revellers, all of them basking in the wonder of a fantastic night that saw the opening of the Olympics.

We stopped over in Chislehurst overnight as it was nearly 2 a.m. by the time we got there. Adam offered to take me on a tour of the village the next day, which I envisaged would be brief, although the idea of Chislehurst Caves and the village having been the home of Napoleon II from 1871 until his death made it sound vaguely historical. I suggested we play it by ear. I mooched around inside Adam's house and found his stereo. I found a nice tune that brought a smile to my tired, yet slightly tipsy and euphoric-after-the-Olympics face and put it on. It was Roberta Flack.

I closed my eyes and started dancing slowly around the living room.

"Hey, mind you don't fall over the coffee table, Fiona", said Adam as he entered the room with two coffee mugs.

"Oh, I'll be okay," I said, giggling, "If you are that worried, dear Adam, then why not come and dance with me!"

Adam put down the mugs and ambled over to me, making an exaggerated demonstration of what he termed 'having as much rhythm as a pregnant catholic', he put his arms around my waist and we moved around the room while I gently sang the song to myself.

"The first time, ever I saw your face..."

Oh feck! I forgot where I was and who I was dancing with and reached up and kissed Adam! Our lips met and I felt a beautiful warmth suddenly envelope me – a warmth that I had not felt in months. I suddenly stopped dancing, opened my eyes and realised where I was. I broke from Adam's embrace, apologised profusely to him and ran to the spare room, sobbing.

Confusion

The next morning you could have cut the atmosphere at breakfast with a knife. To be absolutely fecking honest, Adam didn't say a word, as he was a consummate gentleman. I remained very quiet and ate my breakfast, waiting for Adam to say something, but he didn't say a word.

"Adam, I wanted to apologise for last night."

"Nothing to apologise for."

"I mean it, I don't know what came over me. I didn't want to put you in an impossible situation, I'm sorry..."

"As I said, nothing to apologise for. To be honest it was wonderful but I won't make any comment on it ever again, unless you want to."

"I don't know. I am so fecking confused by all of this!"

"Then be confused for as long as you want, forever if you want. As I said, I won't talk about it if you don't want to, 'kay?" Adam tenderly reached out and, with a single fingertip, lifted my chin so that I could see the sincerity in his eyes. My eyes were not so good, as I had been awake most of the night, worrying about the fecking fool I had made of myself and how I had bespoiled the honour and memory of my late husband. Adam simply winked, and smiled at me. I did my best to smile back at him, and then returned to my tea and toast.

The conversation was a little stilted on our way back to pick up the twins, and from there to Winchelsea Beach. I must say, however, that Adam was true to his word, and he didn't mention what had transpired the night before up in Chislehurst. He stayed for a cup of coffee then said he had to get back – trust me to balls up my friendship with a lovely man by being unable to talk about what was going on in my sodding head! He did say, though, that he'd be in touch soon to finish off the book with me before he started his studies over at Brighton.

Two days later I rang up my bereavement counsellor who, to be honest, I had hardly been in contact with. Sam, who was a very understanding lady, sounded genuinely pleased to hear from me. We arranged an appointment to meet up and talk over a coffee later in the week.

The day of my appointment came and Sam was there, ready to offer advice and, more importantly, listen to my ramblings. She was in her early forties, and had lost her husband in a car crash ten years earlier. It's what I would call the first rule of being a counsellor, being able to empathise with the thoughts and feelings of the person to whom they are listening. That said, Sam had made a conscious decision not to look for a new relationship, so I viewed our meeting with a little trepidation. We sat over a latte and mulled over the situation.

"So what do you want to happen?" Sam was a little blunt in her questioning techniques sometimes.

"Oh feck, Sam, I don't honestly know. I know there is something lovely about spending time with Adam, and he is a genuinely lovely guy, but I don't know if... if I want... no, if I am ready to contemplate a relationship with a new man after Peter's death. Does that make sense?"

"Okay, let's look at this a different way... if you were ready, would you feel able to enter into a relationship with your late husband's brother?"

"Why the feck don't you try me on the easy ones first? Ask me a fecking question on quantum physics, that'll do the trick!" I smiled and immediately put my hand to my forehead, as Sam had hit upon the nub of the problem. If I were ready, only a few months after Peter's death, to enter into a new relationship, how shit would it be to be doing so with his younger brother?

Time would tell, I guess.

Important little details

Well, the days passed and, to be honest, I was still as confused as ever. Adam had done the decent thing in this situation, and had kept in the background, not doing anything to pressure me either way. For that, at least, I was grateful.

I decided I needed a fresh perspective on things, and invited Peter's older children down to lunch. Well, when I say lunch, with my cooking prowess it turned out to be fecking cheese on toast and fish finger sandwiches. Still, it wasn't the food that was important; it was the company and the conversation.

Unfortunately Peter was unwell that day, so only Ellen and my miniature kindred spirit, Lizzy, came to visit. They lavished love and attention on Seamus and the twins, then we sat down over our 'gourmet' lunch and I decided to broach the subject head-on.

"Girls, there's something I need to talk to you about."

"Oooh, what?" Lizzy replied excitedly.

"It's not an easy thing to discuss. It's about feelings and the way my mind is spinning at the moment. I never thought I would need to have this conversation, let alone at the moment, but it seems that I have to. I just don't know how to start the conversation, save to say that you both know that I loved... love your dad intensely and nothing will ever change that..."

"Oh, *that* conversation, "Ellen replied. She had always been less forthright than her little sister, but that is not to say that I didn't value her opinion, "well, Fiona, let's just say that the moment has been prepared for."

She got up from the table and walked into the entrance hall to pick up her coat. She fished around in the inside pocket and pulled out an envelope.

"You remember how dad was always so organised? Well, I think he was *very* organised indeed." She handed me the envelope and indicated for me to remove the letter inside and to read it.

My dearest darlings, Ellen, Lizzy and Peter

I am trying to be the most organised dad in the world here. I am not writing to you about yourselves, but your step-mum, Fiona. There's no need to talk to her about this letter if either there is no need or you don't want to. You will always know that I will leave things like that up to your judgment.

There will come a time, I am sure, when Fiona will start to have feelings about another man. This will not mean, and I mean it, that she has stopped loving me, but there comes a time when all of us need the love and companionship of another being to ensure that life is as happy as possible.

Now I don't normally tell you three darling children what to do, but on this occasion I am. Whether it is three months after my death, or three years, you need to let Fiona live her own life, as it is her future happiness at stake here. I know in my heart that you three will be happy and lead fulfilled lives when you all grow up, but at the moment it is up to you to support Fiona in whatever she chooses to do, as she will do whatever she thinks is right to secure her own happiness and that of your half-brother and half-sister, Dylan and Felicity.

Fiona will never stop loving you, her three lovely stepchildren, but here I am asking you to do what needs to be done, to accept whatever she needs to do to secure her own happiness. You never know, Uncle Adam might split up with that frightful Claudia woman and be available!

I will sign off now, remember that I love each and every one of you and will never stop doing so, even now that I am gone.

Your ever-loving dad xxxxxx

There were tears rolling down my cheeks as I finished reading the letter. I wiped them away with my sleeve as I folded it back up and handed it to Ellen.

"So you knew that this thing might happen before I did?" I asked.

Ellen and Lizzy nodded sagely. Ellen spoke for both of them.

"Fiona, dad is right, you need to do whatever you need to do. It would be wholly selfish of us three to expect you to behave in a certain way just because dad is gone. He's gone but not forgotten, and never will be, but that doesn't mean that life doesn't move on. Love is not some finite resource that has to be shared out sparingly. It grows!"

She got up and gave me a huge hug, the kind of hug that made me sure that she wasn't merely saying those words, but that she, along with her brother and sister, believed every single one of them.

"And besides," added Lizzy, "remember the Latin – *Carpe Diem,* Fish of the Day"

We all of us burst out laughing.

Organisation

I was still unsure about things, even if I seemingly had the children's blessing. I spent the next three days in quiet contemplation of 'the situation', as Eeyore would have termed it, and looked after Felicity and Dylan as well as they had ever been. I decided that, whatever I did, my children would have the best fecking upbringing possible!

I was still not sure about things, and decided to consult the one family friend who I knew would be able to offer me impartial advice, which is why, later that day, I was sitting in the waiting room of the medical centre, waiting to see Dr Matthews, on the pretext of getting a check-up and a repeat prescription for my anti-depressants, which I had subscribed to after my episode with the Jameson's Whiskey and the paracetamol.

"Well, Fiona, how the devil are you?"

"To be honest, doctor, I am confused. First of all, can I have a new prescription for my happy pills?"

"Well, I will need to do some basic checks first. How are those lovely twins?" He checked my blood pressure and performed the other necessary checks.

"So how else can I help you?"

"Well, doctor, it's about an emotional matter. Oh shit, I am so confused." I started sobbing.

"Hey, no need to be a confused wreck. You are getting over the death of your husband, a lovely man with whom you spent all too short a time. And once you start feeling better you will find yourself a new man and who knows what will happen – you're still young!"

I was more than a little exasperated. "Why are you talking to me like this? I am still a grieving widow? I know you can be bloody blunt at times, but can you please offer me a little more sensitivity?"

"I am sorry, Fiona. Maybe something in writing will help? You see, just before he went into the hospice, Peter gave me a letter for safe keeping. He knew that you were, are even, a young woman and eventually the time will come. So let's just say that this moment has been prepared for."

Those words echoed ones that Ellen had said to me only very recently – was I going to find that everything had been thought of by my late beloved Eeyore?

Dr Matthews opened the top drawer of his Victorian-style mahogany desk and pulled out an envelope. Bugger me; I was dreading the sight of these letters. Then my mind was cast back to the coded envelope I had found among Peter's journal jottings. I'd finally worked it all out! That was the answer!

Fiona

Falling In Love?

Call Doctor Matthews!

Peter

Well, it seemed that Peter was prepared for every single bloody eventuality! I took the envelope from Dr Matthews and opened it. He muttered something about 'checking some files' and that he'd be about five minutes.

February 18th 2012

My darling Fiona,

It's strange, but it doesn't feel the slightest bit strange writing this letter to you. What I mean to say is that my situation would appear to be the most heartbreaking that anyone could find themselves in, but I actually feel at peace with the world, at peace, if you can call it that, with Malcolm, and ready to go, as it were.

If you receive this letter it will mean that you have been to see my good friend, and my own favourite GP, Dr Matthews. I have sworn him to secrecy about this letter until the appropriate time arises, as I think you need to complete your own particular grieving process at whatever pace you need, and that itself is something that is peculiar to each and every person.

Even though I am in the latter stages of dying I am not foolish enough, or feeble-minded enough to consider what eventualities may occur in the near, mid or far future. You are now a beautiful woman (stunningly, sexily, gorgeously beautiful I might add) who is only just entering the prime of her life. Thirty years-old is merely the beginning of life, not the end, and just because you are the mother to twin babies does not mean your life is at an end. Our babies, Felicity and Dylan, are the most beautiful double-act that I have ever managed to achieve, and are so radically different from Ellen, Lizzy and Peter that I can happily make them the exception.

You are such a fabulous mother to our two gorgeous little people, and a fabulous step-mum to the other three, that I am certain that nothing will change in those respects no matter what you choose to do with other aspects of your life.

And so, my darling, we come to those other aspects of your life. I do not, I repeat not, expect my young widow to enter a convent, take a vow of celibacy or do a showcase of songs from 'The Sound of Music', or whatever else widows think is expected of them. There will come a time, whether it be three months, six months, three years or thirty years after my death, that you may well find yourself having feelings about another man, and will be in two minds as to what to do about it. You may think you have not been a widow long enough; you may be concerned about what other members of my family will say, or may think that I would be grossly offended and would think you were defiling my memory. Well you know what I am going to say, don't you?

When people do that crazy thing called falling in love, they are falling in love with the person they see before them. If anyone falls in love with you it is not in spite of you being a young widowed mother, it is because of whom you are, the complete package in front of them. We are who we are because of what has happened to us during our passage through life, and that's part of the fun of it, I suppose. We are all of us imperfect, and it is when a person sees our imperfect self as perfect that we know that they are 'the One'.

When you do fall in love again, don't worry about me. I am confident enough to know that your love for me was such that it never dissipated while we were together, and now we are apart, and you must go on living, and find happiness, in whatever form that may take.

I wouldn't dare tell you who you should fall in love with. He, or she even, may be very similar to me or my complete opposite. It could be my kid brother, Adam (sorry I am not in the position to

write him a personal testimonial if he does turn out to be 'the One',
but he's not a bad lad), or even Auntie Maud (she might be a little
old for you, though). Whatever or whomever you choose; I know
you will make the right choice for you, and for Felicity and Dylan.
I will never forget you, and will watch over you and the kids from a
distance. I know you will never forget, but I also will have the
capacity to move on, and that is not a problem.

Love is never finite – that is the key.

Be happy, my love

Peter xxxxx

I cried – not big wet tears of sadness and grief, but warm, soaking ones of happiness, as it felt as if my darling Peter had everything taken care of. He knew this situation might arise and had thought it through. It was odd, but I felt that, even now he had gone, Eeyore was still looking out for me and trying to offer guidance. I wish he were around to tell me in person, but then again, if he were this wouldn't be arising!

Doctor Matthews returned a few minutes later and checked that I was okay. He knew what the letter contained, as apparently Peter had told him about it. Like the sensible man he was, he was true to his word and had not raised the letter's contents with me until I sought him out. Grieving, he told me, was a process that took different people a different amount of time, and that he knew, eventually, that one day I would come to see him. He was particularly pleased that I hadn't taken too long.

"Well, that's one thing fewer I need to worry about before I retire. I am sixty-eight years old now, the letter has been passed, you are fine or, at least, getting there, and your twins are fine and healthy. I can now get my golf clubs out of storage and hit some balls in anger!"

Dr Matthews smiled at me, warmth radiating from his twinkling, ageing eyes.

I got up from my seat and walked over to him, shook him by the hand and then gave him a huge hug and a kiss on the cheek.

"Thanks for everything, doctor. I am still not sure what to do, but at least I know that whatever I actually decide on has Peter's approval. Get a birdie for me, eh?"

Part Four – New Beginnings

Onwards and Upwards

February 2013

Oh feck! This journal is certainly ending in a way that I didn't expect it to. There is so much to compute that things are inherently complex, as always.

It's six months now since I went to see Dr Matthews and he gave me *that* letter, but that is not to say that I have been sitting idly on my arse doing feck all in the meantime. So, where should I start?

Well, first of all I think Felicity and Dylan are first and foremost on the list. They are now a year old and are so much fun to be around! It was a real milestone on Christmas Day. We had a huge family get-together down at Winchelsea Beach. Sheila, Peter's mum, came down to help me with the actual logistics and to show me how to stick my hand up a turkey's arse. I decided that the most important thing was for everyone to get together, friends and 'foes', in-laws and out. Alice and Norman were there with their daughters, and I invited Alex and James along with Ellen, Lizzy and Peter. In fact the only one who wasn't sure he could make it was fecking Adam!

Anyway, as we all sat down to relax after a humungous lunch, we were all amazed to see both Felicity and Dylan slowly pull themselves to their feet whilst holding on to the sofa's edge, teetering for an unsteady step and then landing with a resounding bounce on their arses. Still, they obviously enjoyed it as they looked around at the gathered congregation with huge, beaming, gummy smiles.

All in all it was a perfect day. The only thing missing was the twins' uncle, but who could really blame him? The last time he had really spent some quality time with them was the day after their mummy made a drunken pass at him. I tried to put a brave face on things and get through the day. If he could get in touch, he would do so, is how I kept telling myself.

And so Christmas Day turned into Boxing Day, and then we entered that amazing 'dead time' between the two sets of festivities. It's amazing how slowly those days between Christmas and New Year's seem to go, so slow that you seem to lose track of which day it is for an extended period of time. It seemed poignant to me that the last time I felt like this was the time when Peter was dying. And there, dear reader, I think we have found the turning point. It wasn't tragic any more, it didn't bring me out in howling, uncontrollable sobbing; it was *poignant,* as if something was still there but had lost its power to hurt so intensely. Sure, I still miss Eeyore, and will do every day, but it felt like he was letting me go a bit.

On New Year's Eve I received a text, which in itself was a small fecking miracle, as the mobile signal down here in Winchelsea Beach was normally non-existent. I was a little startled, therefore, when my phone signalled an arriving message.

F

In later?

A

I know I try to be charitable most of the time, but all I could think at that very moment was 'Stuff you, Adam!' Here I was, having contemplated one of the most mind-bogglingly complex things that someone can, namely, working out if I wanted to move on after losing a partner, and all I got was a brief message. No 'How are you?' no 'can we talk?' no 'I'm sorry.'

I had half a mind to reply 'No, feck off!' but then part of me thought that I would really like to see Adam, no matter what had happened in July last year, so I replied to his text saying I would be at home and not out painting Winchelsea Beach a shade of pale pink in search of general debauchery. Adam sent a reply telling me not to worry about food as he had everything sorted. Well, that's a fecking relief, I thought.

I heard Adam's car roll up to the house at about 8 p.m. He seemed a little quiet as I welcomed him at the door. He gave me a perfunctory hug and asked me if I had had a pleasant Christmas with all the family. Do we really need all this small talk, I thought. Adam 'set to' in the kitchen and decided that a Thai red chicken curry was in order, with sticky boiled rice and a bottle of something chilled. He asked me if I was able to manage making a salad accompaniment! Cheeky fecker!

We sat and chatted over dinner, and we still hadn't got to the nub of the issue, as I decided to think of it. It wasn't so much an elephant in the room as a full-grown woolly mammoth. Could we continue as if nothing had happened on the night of the Olympics' Opening Ceremony? Did we want to? Did Adam want to? There was only one thing that was certain and that was that I didn't have a fecking clue what I wanted.

I washed up and then Adam and I sat down to listen to some music and to chat, and this time hopefully about something more pressing.

"So, how have you been keeping these last few months, Fiona?"

"Oh, you know. Children, paperwork, art, you, more paperwork, the life of a merry widow!"

The fecker didn't bat an eyelid. Either he was playing things amazingly coolly or the bastard was thick as forty-eight short planks.

"You're probably wondering why I haven't contacted you, aren't you?" Well ding-dong – welcome to the party, Mr Robbins. Have a prize for finally bloody well coming to the party and catching on!

Adam explained that there had been a number of reasons for the continued radio silence. Firstly and, I admit, understandably, he had been up to his ears in training to be a teacher. Lectures, essays, and reading hefty tomes on the latest snippets of educational theory – it had all taken its toll. There had been other reasons, though.

"To be absolutely honest, Fiona, I have been trying to get my head around it all."

"What do you mean by *it all*?"

"You know, me, you, us, Peter, the twins, Ellen, Lizzy, Peter, mum, and Uncle Tom Cobbley and all, I guess. I've been mixed up and mulling it over, I guess."

"You've been mixed up? I have been trying to get over drunkenly trying to seduce you. I couldn't work out whether it was the drink acting, my hormones out of control or my psyche trying to tell me something."

"So are we saying we have both been sitting thirty-five miles apart, both contemplating and ruminating and doing nothing about it?"

"That pretty much sums it all up, yes! For Christ's sake, Adam. I am still unsure what my mind is saying, but let's at least just bloody well talk about it, yeah?"

"Sounds good to me. Tell you what though; Pete would have called us both a pair of daft dickheads, wouldn't he?" Adam attempted to chuckle.

"I guess so, although I am not in possession of a dick, so I will have to join in with you in spirit!" We both started laughing. "I think I am now enough of an experienced widow to know that he'd tell me to go with the flow. I guess I am just, sort of... scared."

"Scared of what? My incredible sexual prowess?" That made me splutter, then I noticed he was winking.

"No, you silly beggar! If I were to put it into words then I would say I am scared of what the family will think."

"Oh bugger the family! Well, not all of them, as Auntie Maud would be a bit of a challenge. I think I have sorted out my head enough to put it into words. I think you are lovely. You are beautiful, warm, happy and you are a fabulous person to be around. You are normally chipper and your sense of the absurd is divine – it's just like Pete's was."

Adam took a sip of his wine and continued.

"What I am trying to say, Fi is... may I call you Fi?" I nodded my assent and told him to bloody well get on with it. "Well, what I am trying to say is that if you were to decide that you wanted to become romantically involved with me I would feel honoured and privileged. I would be with you because it is you, a lovely wonderful and, if I might be so bold, sexy woman, and not because you are my elder brother's widow. Does that make sense?"

"So are you trying to say that it's because I am me, and not because of my circumstances?"

"Precisely. Now I might add that, if nothing comes of it, I will not mind in the least. I might slightly regret what might have been, but I will understand fully."

"Adam, I understand totally. It's a bit of a fecking mess but, if we want, we can sort something out. Have you heard from Claudia lately?"

"Ah well, I did get a Christmas Card. She's taken up with a docker from Bremerhafen and, apparently, he is reaching the parts that mere mortals like myself cannot reach."

"Ooh, not nice! Well, very nice, if she gets the chance! Oops, I'm sorry!" I blushed at what was simultaneously a possible insult to Adam's manhood and an admission that I, perhaps, was beginning to miss intimate contact with a man.

"Well, that's just charming!" I could, though, tell that this was *faux* outrage, as there was a sparkle in Adam's eye. I got up out of my armchair and put some music on. It was a little bit of Wilson Pickett. I suggested to Adam that we try to dance and see if we could behave ourselves. Adam agreed and got up to join me.

He placed his hands around my waist, resting the heel of each palm on my hips, with his fingertips gently placed around my back. I put my arms around his neck, and we danced. As the music progressed I placed my cheek on Adam's chest, and could feel two things coming through to my face. Firstly, a very intense, strong heartbeat, and secondly a warmth that I had not felt in many a day. I moved myself instinctively closer to him, so that our bodies were touching. Adam reached up and stroked my hair, and then kissed the top of my head. I looked up at this man, and asked him a question.

"Adam, may I kiss you?"

"Let me think now. Yes, I think that is in order." I reached up and kissed him. It was a long way to go, as he was even taller than Peter was. Our lips met, and I melted into his arms. The music stopped, but we continued. He put his arms around me and led me to the bedroom.

Afterword

Contrary to what you might expect, we didn't make love that night. Adam, took me to my room, dutifully waited around looking at anything possible except me while I got undressed and ready for bead, which included reading a DIY manual, and then, when I was safely ensconced under the duvet, he returned to look at me. There was definitely a family likeness between him and Peter but, as he was seven years Peter's junior his face looked slightly less weathered and he still had most of his hair. He looked at me intently, not staring, but in a caring, attentive manner.

"Are you going to join me under this duvet?" I asked him.

"We'll see. It's not that I am declining your very kind offer, but if something becomes of us we'll have plenty of time for that kind of business".

Adam and I spent the next hour or so talking about all manner of things. We chatted, and kissed, and kissed and chatted. As the first fireworks of the New Year were let off he reached over and kissed me warmly.

"Happy New Year, Fi"

"Happy New Year, Mister Robbins!" I lay my head against his chest and he stroked my hair, gently, but in a way that I knew he was there. We chatted some more until I fell into a contented slumber, and what was to be the best night's sleep I had had in almost a year.

I awoke the next morning to find that I was still in Adam's arms. He was still looking down at me, smiling.

"Good Morning, Fi. Did you sleep well?"

"You don't know how well! How long have you been looking at me sleeping?"

"For an instant, and an eternity." This reminded me so much of Peter, and I smiled contentedly.

I gave him a slight dig in the ribs and smiled to show that I wasn't outraged. I gave a sigh of content.

Suddenly there was the sound of stirring in the nursery.

"You wait there, I'll see what's up". He got up and walked into the children's bedroom. I could hear him talking to Felicity and Dylan in such a calm, soothing manner that anyone would have thought he was a dab hand at this. He changed each nappy in turn and then brought them both in to see their mummy.

"Happy New Year, my darlings!" I said to my fantastic children as Adam placed them in my arms. As I got myself in a position to give them their morning feed, Adam said he'd go and make something for breakfast. He returned a few minutes later with croissants, bread, cheese, coffee and orange juice. He placed the tray in front of me and took the children off my hands.

"What do you want to do today, then?"

"Well, we could go out for a walk?" I suggested.

"Okay then. Where shall we go for a walk?"

"I think I know..."

Later that morning we loaded up the Voyager with children and all the accompanying bits of baby paraphernalia and set off. I directed Adam through Hastings, along the coast through Bexhill on Sea, and through Eastbourne. Eventually we parked up in the car park up at Beachy Head, where I had met my dear darling Eeyore a lifetime and a minute before. I don't know why but it seemed fitting to visit this beautiful spot on New Year's Day.

We walked along the grass with the twin baby buggy and Seamus in tow, hands by our sides. Suddenly our fingers brushed one another, and then my fingers instinctively looked to link with those of Adam, and the next thing you knew we were fecking well holding hands. And you know what? It didn't feel in the least bit unnatural. We turned to one another, and kissed for what seemed like an hour.

I asked Adam to walk with the buggies for a second while I stood on the cliff. I took off the necklace that Peter had given me on that ever-so eventful daytrip to France, looked at it, and looked out to sea. I then kissed the necklace and placed it on my pocket, finally patting the pocket for good measure.

The pub up at Beachy Head is okay for coffee or a drink and a bite to eat, but as a place for a date I wouldn't rate it. We sat and had a latte with the children and Seamus and then decided to drive back along the back roads to Winchelsea Beach. We loaded the children and the dog back into the car, and then we stood there, facing each other. We did what seemed to be the most natural thing in the world, and that was to have a full-on, passionate, red-blooded snogfest. The kind of thing that my dearly departed late husband would have termed as 'slug wrestling'.

Eventually we both came up for air. The only thing I could hear was what I thought was Peter's voice, saying 'About bloody time!'

We drove back northwards, through Polegate and through Hailsham, Herstmonceux and from there into St Leonards and past Fairlight to Winchelsea Beach. The frustrating thing, though, was that, even if we wanted to, we couldn't get up to much with the twins being awake. We kissed and cuddled on the sofa while the children played in their cots, and also we played together as... oh shit... I almost said 'as a family' there. It's these little things that I find myself thinking, or saying, or writing, that suddenly bring me up to a shuddering halt, before I continue my way along the road I seem to be headed on.

I'd better get this sorted, I thought, as, as seemed to be a natural progression from the current situation, things might lose their heat if I suddenly call Adam 'Peter' whilst we are being intimate! And then again, if I spend my time worrying about that, I might never feel like making love ever again. Oh feck!

That evening we bathed, fed and put the children to bed, and then Adam and I prepared something light to eat. I wasn't all that hungry, mainly as I was preoccupied with what might or might not happen if I got intimate with my brother-in-law. As I was washing up the dinner things I was pre-empted. Adam had come up close behind me and had tenderly kissed my neck. He put his arms around my waist.

I couldn't resist, I turned round and covered his face in warm, soapy water, clasping his face and kissing him passionately. It was like my passion was being set free.

What happened next I will not divulge, even to my closest friends. A while later, we were lying in bed, holding each other. I decided to break the silence.

"Adam, you're not going to bugger off out of here now, are you?"

"Of course not. What makes you think that?"

"History, I guess – divorce, widowhood, the only thing left for me on my 'relationship bingo' card is 'dumped after a shag'."

Adam kissed my head, just as Peter used to do. I decided to add to the emotional turmoil, mainly because I am a masochist.

"That pleases me. I had better warn you, though. If we do stay with one another for a good while, having children is not an option, after the car crash, you know."

"That's okay. Two's company, three's a recipe for insomnia!" He kissed me again, and I slowly drew my fingertip up from his knee to the inside of his thigh. Adam gave an involuntary moan and I climbed on top of him.

Today is the first anniversary of the death of my husband, Peter Robbins. I am now happily in a relationship with his brother, Adam Robbins, and the most momentous thing about today, apart from the poignancy of the date, is the fact that my life is filled with hope, not guilt.

I have one more letter to sort out and then it's time to go back to that song Ellen was thinking of a year ago: 'Tomorrow? Who knows?"

Monday 25th March 2013

Dearest Eeyore,

I didn't think I would ever feel the need to write to you about this, but I am going to quote that politician who was asked why bad things were happening to his government. His answer was 'events, dear boy, events!'

This is going to sound remarkably like a 'Dear John' letter, but please let me assure you it's not.

I will never forget meeting you, my darling, Peter, more than a year ago up at Beachy Head, and I will treasure all the things you have given me – friendship, hope and security as well as bring some wonderful people into my life – your mum, your three children, Auntie Maud, Alice and Adam. Of course I cannot forget the constant reminders of the wonderful man to whom I was married, our children, Felicity and Dylan. They are turning into a right pair of personalities, my love, and I love spending so much time with them. Dylan is starting to look like you, I think, although he has more hair! Both of them delight in silliness and absurdity (I wonder where they get that from).

Now, I need to take issue with you, my darling, but just a little bit. I wasn't aware at all that you knew me so well. When I was deep in the dark days of a widow's grief, if anyone had spoken to me about 'moving on' I would have told them to 'feck off' resoundingly, but as the months went on I needed to get my head straight, I guess. We used the phrase 'getting your shit together' so much when you were alive, and I am living proof that there are all different kinds of shit to deal with in life. It was all so confusing then.

Well, to be honest, I think it still is, but the misty confusing moments are now fewer and farther between.

And then I have to take issue with the fact that, basically, you bloody well knew that I would end up with Adam! I tell you what; if you can come up with a set of lottery numbers I would be most grateful.

For one thing, I do have to thank you. Thank you for sending Adam that letter to drop in. If he hadn't I wouldn't be able to love our babies in the way that they deserve, or take my life to a different stage.

I wish you wouldn't write codes, though, as my mind was a complete mess when I went to see Dr Matthews (he's happily retired and swinging his niblick like a demon), but your letter, and the one that you sent Ellen, Lizzy and Peter (yes, they showed it to me), showed me that you knew I would get to this stage.

So what stage am I at now? Well, I think you could say that I have been 'with' Adam since New Year's Day. He is kind and gentle and has a wonderful way with Felicity and Dylan. One thing is for sure, and that is that if Adam and I do become a permanent fixture, and at the moment that is my hope, he will only ever be a step-daddy to the children. They are, and only ever will be, the children of Mr Peter Robbins and Mrs Fiona Robbins – that is non-negotiable. Then again, you know Adam and know that he would never contemplate anything different anyway.

So there we have it, my darling. I am not in a 'happy place', but I do have peace and contentment. As for the future? Well, all I can say is that the plan is to remain content and to take life as it comes. You and you alone, gave me the strength to take whatever life throws at me and to stick a defiant digit up to it, showing that I *can cope, but then again, not cope, as what I and the children will do is thrive.*

It is an absolute privilege to be your widow, my love, but it is also a privilege to have been given the opportunity to have you in my life, in which you will remain, no matter what the outcome of the future is. The important thing is that you know, understand, and approve.

I will sign off now. I may send you the odd letter in the future when I need a little bit of guidance on a matter, as you now have access to the wisest minds in history. While you are at it, could you ask Fanie Craddock how I can make the perfect soufflé?

I love you, now and forever. I'm signing off now, though, to live the rest of my life.

Neef xxxxx